"I was your firs... as if she needed the reminder.

"I taught you about passion, what it could mean, how deeply it could run. I don't believe a woman ever forgets such an experience, no matter what might come later."

"She doesn't forget being dumped, either! I remember you grew tired of me rather quickly."

"But I've never forgotten how you felt in my arms—so fragile and unsure. I remember the texture of your skin, your hair...your touch, your scent...."

Determined to extricate herself from a situation growing more unbearable by the second, she stood up. "And I just remembered the time."

Her legs were shaking, but the fear that she'd collapse in a heap at his feet was the least of her worries. Her brain, on the other hand, was a matter for serious concern. It seemed incapable of stemming the rush of words spilling out of her mouth, regardless of how indiscreet they might be. Already she was lying to him, and the longer she remained there, the greater the chance that she'd lie again—and again.

Some people know practically from birth that they're going to be writers. CATHERINE wasn't one of them. Her first idea was to be a nun, which was clearly never going to work! A series of other choices followed. She considered becoming a veterinarian (but she lacked the emotional stamina to deal with sick and injured animals), a hairdresser (until she overheated a curling iron and singed about five inches of hair off the top of her best friend's head the day before her first date) or a nurse (but that meant emptying bedpans—eee-yew!). As a last resort, she became a high school English teacher, and loved it.

Eventually, she married, had four children and, always, always, a dog or two or three. How can a house become a home without a dog? she asks. How does an inexperienced mother cope with babies, if she doesn't have a German Shepherd nanny?

In time, the children grew up and moved out on their own—as children are wont to do, regardless of their mother's pleading that they will remain babies who don't mind being kissed in public! She returned to teaching, but a middle-aged restlessness overtook her and she looked for a change of career.

What's an English teacher's area of expertise? Well, novels, among other things, and moody, brooding, unforgettable heroes: Heathcliff, Edward Fairfax Rochester, Romeo and Rhett Butler. Then there's that picky business of knowing how to punctuate and spell, and the "rules" of sentence structure and how to break them for dramatic effect. They all pointed her in the same direction: breaking the rules every chance she got, and creating her own moody, brooding unforgettable heroes. And where do they belong? In Harlequin Presents books, of course, which is where she happily resides now.

THE ITALIAN'S SECRET CHILD
CATHERINE SPENCER

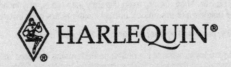

HARLEQUIN®

TORONTO • NEW YORK • LONDON
AMSTERDAM • PARIS • SYDNEY • HAMBURG
STOCKHOLM • ATHENS • TOKYO • MILAN • MADRID
PRAGUE • WARSAW • BUDAPEST • AUCKLAND

This book is dedicated to my seven-month-old Labrador
Retriever, Beau, who liked it so much that he ate the
diskette, the day before it was due on my editor's desk.

ISBN-13: 978-0-373-82044-3
ISBN-10:   0-373-82044-5

THE ITALIAN'S SECRET CHILD

First North American Publication 2006.

Copyright © 2004 by Spencer Books Limited.

www.eHarlequin.com

Printed in U.S.A.

CHAPTER ONE

THE man emerged from a clump of trees about twenty yards away, at the junction of a paved walkway leading to the villa next door, and the gravel path coiling down the cliff to the beach. Even at that distance, and with the late sun dazzling her vision enough to distort his image, something about him—the proud tilt of his head, perhaps, or the lean and stealthy elegance of his stride—stirred such a sense of familiarity in Stephanie that she gasped aloud. Then, fearful that he might have heard, she pressed a hand to her mouth, darted behind a tall plant hung with huge trumpet-shaped flowers, and peered cautiously between its broad leaves.

Of course, it couldn't be *him*. It was her imagination playing fast and loose with her common sense because she was in Italy. *His* country, *his* language, *his* culture. Which was pretty absurd, she decided, when her thumping heart slowed enough to allow her to think rationally. *He*'d been from Tuscany, from a small town on the Ligurian coast, and spent his days in the mountains, quarrying the world-famous Carrara marble. A plain working man who, even during his brief summer sojourn in Canada, wore dusty blue jeans and sweat-streaked T-shirts.

But she was on Ischia, an island in the Bay of Naples, over three hundred miles south, as the crow flies, from Carrara, and a lifetime removed from when she spent summers at her grandparents' house at Bramley-On-The-Lake. And the man in the wheat-colored slacks and white shirt, profiled against the indigo sea and standing with one long leg braced against an outcropping of rock, looked

5

nothing like a laborer. Rather, he resembled one of the rich Italians who'd shunned tourist-infested Capri, and chosen instead this small and lovely island for his summer retreat.

True. Definitely all true. But that hardly entitled him to trespass on the private property leased by her grandparents. So why was she lurking behind a protective screen of lush vegetation, when she'd have been entirely within her rights to accost him openly and demand an explanation for his presence?

Because he'd sent a kaleidoscope of pictures from her past spinning through her mind, that's why! Memories so staggering in their clarity of color and scent and taste that her skin prickled. They flooded her senses, conjuring up the hot Ontario summer she'd turned nineteen when, day after day, the temperature hovered close to forty degrees Celsius, and the nights were so humid and airless, a person couldn't sleep.

In her mind's eye, she saw again the dust motes twirling idly in the finger beams of sunlight slanting through the open door of her grandparents' stables, and *him*, stripped to the waist, his bronzed torso gleaming. As if it had happened just yesterday, she recalled the terrified thrill of sneaking from the house in the dead of night, and climbing the ladder to the hayloft. Felt again the horse blanket against her bare back as she lay beneath him, with only a sprinkling of stars to see how willingly she gave herself to a man six years older, and a lifetime more experienced.

Echoes of a voice deeply seductive, intriguingly foreign, floated hauntingly across the mists of time. She heard his murmured entreaties, her own broken, inarticulate sighs of acquiescence. For a brief moment of insanity, she relived the stolen hours of passion, the pulsing strength of his body, the puckering anticipation of hers. And then, before she could wrestle herself free of it, the memory of his rejection burst over her in a great bubble of pain that bruised her heart all over again.

Weak and shaking, she sank to her knees. Spreading her palms flat on the sun-baked earth, she forced herself to take long, steadying breaths. Willed her pulse to stop racing. And slowly...slowly...the present swam back into focus. The sharp scent of lemons snuffed out the smell of hay, and horses, and...sex. The glowing peach-colored blossoms swaying before her face blotted out the pale wash of moonlight on naked limbs.

What a fool, to allow the most painful period of her life to rise up and take hold after so many years, all because, on the day she arrived in Italy, a man with black hair and broad shoulders happened to cross her line of vision! If so insignificant an occurrence could reduce her to a heap of cowering flesh, she'd likely be a raving idiot by month's end. And that, most certainly, was not the reason she'd flown, with her son, from Canada's west coast to this volcanic speck of land in the Tyrrhenian Sea.

Consider it less a request than an order, her Grandmother Leyland's letter had stated with rare asperity. *Brandon and I will have been married sixty-five years on July 12th, which is a long time by anyone's standards and surely deserving of extraordinary recognition. However, we absolutely forbid your marking the occasion with any material token, and ask instead for something you perhaps will find more difficult to give. We want our family to join us in Italy for the entire month of July. The various estrangements between our son and grandchildren have lasted long enough. My beloved husband's health is failing and I'm determined that he enjoy whatever time remains to him, knowing that you've made a serious attempt at reconciling your differences. In light of his unconditional love toward every one of you, from the moment you drew your first breath, satisfying this one demand, as he grows closer to his last, is the very least you can offer him now, and if that smacks of emotional blackmail, then so be it. At my age, a woman does what she has to do, without apology or embarrassment.*

She should possess one tenth of her grandmother's grit! Mortified by her weakness, Stephanie got to her feet and peeped again through the leaves of the plant. The man had disappeared; had either climbed down the cliff to the beach, or passed under the pergola covered with brilliant pink and red flowers, which connected the villa's gardens with the neighboring grounds.

Cautiously, she emerged from her hiding place and stole forward. Ventured a glance to the left, where the walkway began, and saw nothing. Inched toward the top of the cliff and scanned the path snaking down to the pristine curve of sand at its base, and found it uninhabited. Indeed, the landscape was so palpably deserted, she half wondered if he'd been nothing but a figment of her imagination.

Yet the sense that, all the evidence to the contrary, she was not as alone as it seemed, left her looking back uneasily toward the villa. Its creamy stucco walls, rising up the hillside in a series of graceful arches topped by a blue tiled roof, drowsed in the late afternoon sun. But although the exterior of the house shimmered in the heat, in the room where Simon napped, exhaustion having at last overcome his excitement, the air conditioner kept him cool and comfortable.

"Let him rest now, then he'll be refreshed enough to stay up later than usual tonight," her grandmother had urged, when Stephanie had questioned the wisdom of letting him sleep so long. "It's never too soon to introduce a child to the finer points of gracious living. We'll dine *al fresco* at eight, and dress gloriously for the occasion.

Go explore the gardens, darling girl, and leave me to keep an eye on your boy.''

Stephanie had been glad to escape—not from Simon or her grandparents, nor even her mother and second brother, Andrew, but from her father and eldest brother, Victor. Their incessant and overt disapproval never stopped. It had been nearly seven years since she'd spent any time with them, yet they'd barely paused long enough to say ''Hello'' before they started in with the criticism.

''Tragic that Charles passed away so young,'' her father observed, referring to her ex-husband's untimely demise, five years earlier, ''but at least something good came out of it insofar as you now possess a smattering of respectability.''

''*Respectability?*'' Sincerely puzzled, she'd stared at him. ''How does Charles' dying make me more respectable?''

''You can now claim to be a widow,'' Victor had supplied, adopting the kind of tone one might use in trying to housebreak a backward puppy. ''In case you weren't aware, we don't divorce in this family, Stephanie. It simply isn't done.''

''Really?'' She'd sucked in an affronted breath. ''Well, how convenient of Charles to shuffle off and spare you the stigma of having to call a spade a spade!''

''We're hardly glad the man's dead,'' her father said loftily, his reproving gaze following Simon as he charged excitedly across the terrace to the garden. ''But that boy of yours needs a man's firm hand, a proper role model. If Charles had lived, he'd have remained a positive influence in his son's life. Instead, he chose to work in India and was dead of some obscure disease within six months. What did you do, that he went to such extreme lengths to get away from you?''

Admitted I'd made a mistake in thinking we could make

a go of marriage, she could have replied, *whereas you'd stay miserably shackled to someone throughout eternity if you had to, because maintaining appearances matters to you above all else. As for Charles, he actually isn't Simon's father, which is why he found it so easy to walk away from him.*

But she didn't say any of it, even though part of her would have loved seeing the expression on their faces, had she dared be so outspoken. She'd been brought up to understand that people...*women*...didn't question the wise dictates of the almighty Professors Leyland Senior and Junior, and they certainly didn't blurt out information guaranteed to spatter the family name with scandal.

So she'd kept her mouth shut and in doing so, perpetuated the deceit she'd started almost ten years earlier. At least that way, she could continue to give Simon some sense of family, even though he seldom saw his relatives, because if her father had suspected for a minute that his only grandson was the illegitimate result of a summer affair, he'd have refused to acknowledge him.

Even Stephanie's mother didn't know the truth. Not that Vivienne wouldn't have been sympathetic, but the burden of keeping such a secret from a husband who'd dominated her life from the day she'd said "I do," would have weighed too heavily on her conscience.

Better by far for Stephanie to preserve the *status quo,* and on the surface at least, to act the compliant, respectful daughter. They were all together as a family for only one month, and for her to speak her mind would create precisely the kind of strife her grandparents specifically wanted to avoid. They neither needed nor deserved to have her upset the apple cart. It was balanced precariously enough already.

Still, the undercurrents of that earlier confrontation lingered, making Stephanie reluctant to return to the villa a moment sooner than she had to. Instead, since the interloper she'd seen was long gone, she searched for a spot where she might sit and simply soak in the peaceful ambience of the garden, with its glorious riot of flowers and spectacular view.

She found just the place, a stone bench tucked in a nook, against a backdrop of trailing vines. It offered a perfect look out over the Bay of St. Angelo to the Isle of Capri. Brushing aside a drift of fallen petals, she sat down, blew at the tendrils of hair sticking damply to her forehead, and let the sheer beauty of the setting soak into her consciousness.

Despite her reservations and the unresolved issues with her father, she was glad she'd agreed to come here. It was good for Simon to see something of the world, and it had been years since she'd taken a whole month away from work to be with him. He was growing up so fast; had turned nine on May 28th and was already showing signs of independence. It wouldn't be long before he didn't want to spend so much time with his mother.

Movement to her right had her swinging around nervously, but it was only a butterfly, a gorgeous creature, fluttering to land on the rim of a stone urn crammed with some fragrant yellow flower. "You startled me," she said softly. "I thought I was quite alone."

A shadow fell across the path, and an unmistakable, unforgettable voice announced, "Then before arriving at such a conclusion, you should have conducted a more thorough search, instead of assuming that because you could not see me, *I* could not see *you*. How are you, Stephanie?"

Waves of nausea swept over her, leaving her lightheaded with shock. How else to explain that the only word to escape her was a wheezy, agonized, *"Simon!"*

"Dio, but you know how to deflate a man's pride!" he

exclaimed, amusement layering his voice like melted chocolate. "Did I make so fleeting an impression on you, all those years ago, that you don't even remember my name?"

If only! "Matteo De Luca," she stammered faintly, staring at her feet because to look him in the eye would have undone her completely. "What in heaven's name are you doing here?"

"I live here...some of the time."

Her glance flickered sideways, to the villa whose stucco walls had turned apricot in the rays of the setting sun. "Not there."

"Next door, then," he said. "In the gardener's cottage."

That, at least, made some sort of sense in a world gone suddenly crazy. "You're no longer in the quarry business?"

"I have many interests. Marble is but one of them. Who's Simon? Your husband?"

"I'm not married," she said, still evading his gaze, although she could feel it burning the crown of her head. Then, realizing the questions her answer might provoke, added hurriedly, "But I was."

"Yes," he said, a hint of ice glazing his words. "I heard."

His answer surprised her into daring to look him in the face. He was every bit as beautiful as she remembered. "How? Who told you such a thing?"

"Your grandmother. Did you not know we've kept in touch all these years?"

Dear God! What else did he know? "No," she said, amazed and more than a little awed at the composure she managed to project. "She probably realized it wasn't of interest to me."

"I daresay you're right. At the time, I thought it remarkable how soon you replaced me with another man."

"Resilience is one of the benefits of youth, Matteo," she said. "I took your advice to heart and moved on. What did you expect? That I'd spend the rest of my life lamenting your defection?"

"No. I didn't flatter myself quite to that extent."

He should have! She'd never stopped mourning him, never really moved on. Just given the impression that she had, because hiding her wounds had been the only way they had a hope of healing. "What about you?" she asked. "Did you marry?"

He bathed her in a slow smile. "To quote you, *cara,* what had I to offer, that any woman would want me?"

The face of an angel…the body of a god…a mouth that made sin seem respectable, and modesty a liability! Feeling herself flush, Stephanie looked away again. "I suppose you're still too young to know what commitment's all about."

"And you're able to arrive at so damning a conclusion because…?"

Defensively, she said, "Well, what are you now, Matteo? Thirty-two, thirty-three?"

"Thirty-five."

As if she wasn't perfectly aware of that! As if his birth date wasn't etched in her memory as thoroughly as Simon's, or her own! "And still unattached. I guess you're just a late bloomer—one of those men who takes longer than most to mature."

"Or perhaps I'm one of those men who waits until he knows for sure what he wants, before leaping into marriage. I'm not a great believer in divorce."

"You sound just like my father."

"I never thought to hear you admit to such a possibility," he said. "Indeed, I distinctly recall your telling me that, in my raw, untutored state, I had no hope of measuring up to his rarified standards.''

Her flush deepened, this time from shame. "I was barely nineteen, at the time. A girl still, very much influenced by upbringing and my father's expectations of me.''

"You were a woman in all the ways that counted, Stephanie.''

The way he pronounced her name, accenting the first syllable and drawing out the last, caressed her nerve endings with sensuous pleasure. "No," she said, flatly refusing to allow such an untoward response and invoking, instead, the utter lack of feeling with which he'd let her know their affair was over. "I was a silly, naive teenager who thought that when a man said *I love you,* he actually meant it, when in fact what he really wanted was to get her into his bed. You knew how to flatter me, and I didn't know enough to recognize that's all you were doing.''

"All?" His voice dropped to a purr, and she flinched as if he'd touched her. "You did not come to me willingly? I dragged you from your house and brought you to the stable by force?" He shook his head. "That's not how I remember it, *cara.* As I recall, you found much pleasure with me.''

"Did I?" Languidly, she turned her gaze on the blue expanse of sea, feigning utter boredom with the topic. "It's possible, I suppose, so I won't argue the point. But if you want the truth, Matteo, I barely remember the details of our association. I'm afraid they were buried long ago under more significant events in my life.''

"I was your first lover," he said—as if she needed the reminder! "I might not have been fit to sit at your father's table, but I taught you about passion, what it could mean, how deeply it could run. I don't believe a woman ever forgets such an experience, no matter what might come later.''

"She doesn't forget being dumped, either! I remember you grew tired of me rather quickly."

"But I've never forgotten how you felt in my arms— so fragile and unsure. I remember the texture of your skin, your hair...your touch, your scent...."

Determined to extricate herself from a situation growing more unbearable by the second, she stood up. "And I just remembered the time."

Her legs were shaking, but the fear that she'd collapse in a heap at his feet was the least of her worries. Her brain, on the other hand, was a matter for serious concern. It seemed incapable of stemming the rush of words spilling out of her mouth, regardless of how indiscreet they might be. Already, she was lying to him, and the longer she remained there, the greater the chance that she'd lie again—and again.

She couldn't live like that anymore. She wouldn't.

"It was nice seeing you again, Matteo," she said firmly, "but I really must be going."

She made to push by him but, to her horror, he detained her by wrapping his long fingers around her wrist. "You still haven't told me who Simon is."

Ah! The breath pinched in her lungs at the one question she most dreaded. She glanced down at his hand on her arm. To her, at that moment, it represented dark male strength pitted against feminine weakness. At last, on a tiny squeaking sigh of defeat, she said the only thing she could say. "He's my son."

In all conscience, what other choice had she? Matteo was bound to learn the truth eventually, and even if he weren't, she wasn't about to deny her own child.

"Son?" His eyebrows rose.

"Don't look so surprised," she replied, tweaking the truth just enough to throw him off the scent. "My marriage might not have lasted, but at least something good came out of it.''

"Not quite good enough to prevent a divorce, it would seem."

"It's not a child's job to act as the glue holding a couple together."

He lifted his shoulders, his shrug saying plainly enough, even before he spoke, what he thought of her line of reasoning. "No. That responsibility rests squarely on the shoulders of the parents, and I'd have thought having a child would be reason enough to work at saving a marriage."

"It isn't always possible. Some marriages are too fatally flawed."

He shrugged again. "If I had a son—"

"Well, you don't!" she snapped, and could have cut out her tongue. She sounded as shrill as a fishwife, and far more jittery than the conversation warranted. "At least," she went on, moderating her tone, "I assume you don't?"

"No." His eyes, so dark a brown they were almost black, settled reflectively on her face. "But if I had, I would move heaven and earth to keep my marriage intact. I would not allow my child to be torn between his parents, as if he were just another asset to be divided down the middle."

Up at the villa, a small figure stepped onto the terrace and scanned the garden. Recognizing Simon, and terribly afraid that he'd come racing down the path to meet her, she said, "In a perfect world, neither would I, but I learned a long time ago that perfection is seldom within reach. And now, if you'll excuse me—"

"Mom?" Simon called out.

"I'll be right with you, sweetie." She smiled and

waved at him, then turned back to the man at her side and said grimly, "Take your hand off my arm, Matteo. Now!"

But he seemed barely aware of her, and was staring instead at Simon. "So that's your son?"

"Yes."

"I hope I'll get to meet him soon."

Not if she had anything to say about it! "It's possible."

"More than that, it's highly probable. As next door neighbors, we'll likely see quite a bit of one another over the next few weeks." Idly, he pressed his fingers to her inner wrist. "Your pulse is racing, Stephanie. Do I make you nervous?"

"Not in the slightest. But you *are* beginning to annoy me!"

He lowered his lashes, as if to cover up the amused disbelief dancing in his eyes, and raised her hand to his lips. "If you say so," he murmured. "*A presto, cara.* See you soon."

She fervently hoped not, but knew there was little chance she'd get her wish. The most she could be grateful for was that Simon had blue eyes and was blond like her, even though his hair was a shade or two darker. He bore no resemblance at all to Matteo, and no one looking at them would for a moment suspect the two were father and son.

The bickering and backbiting of its residents having finally petered out, the villa lay blanketed by the heavy silence of night. In the room adjoining hers, Simon sprawled in his bed, long ago asleep. But Stephanie, too restless to settle, paced the narrow balcony outside her bedroom, and wondered whatever had possessed her to think, for one moment, that her family was capable of spending more than an hour together before the in-fighting began.

Not that they resorted to raising voices or hurling dishes at one another. Heaven forbid they should so far forget themselves as to behave in a manner unbefitting the descendants of statesmen on both sides of the Canada-U.S. border! Instead, they delighted in sly, hurtful innuendo; in nasty little digs that slipped past a person's guard as stealthily as a knife sliding between the ribs.

Simon had inadvertently started tonight's incident, midway through dinner. "Who was that man you were talking to this afternoon, Mom?" he'd piped up, between the main course and dessert, and that's all it had taken for the rest of the meal to go down the tubes in fine style.

"He lives in the cottage next door," she'd said. "I ran into him while I was exploring the garden."

"Why was he holding your hand?"

Dismally aware of all eyes swiveling in her direction, Stephanie had touched her napkin to her mouth and done her best to contain the flush threatening to lay waste to her composure. "He wasn't *holding* my hand, Simon. He was shaking it. We were just saying hello again because we first met a long time ago."

"A somewhat far-fetched coincidence, meeting him again now, wouldn't you say?" Her father, ever the dignified professor quizzing a delinquent student, ever the disapproving parent saddled with a rebel daughter instead of a third, perfect son, had inspected her suspiciously over the top of his gold-rimmed glasses.

She'd held his gaze. "But true, nevertheless."

Not liking the defiance he heard in her voice, he'd raised his brows in silent reproof. "Indeed? And does this man have a name?"

"Of course he does, Victor," her grandfather said. "It's Matteo De Luca."

"And that's supposed to mean something to me?"

"It should. He came over from Italy and spent almost

six weeks with us, the summer Stephanie graduated high school. He bought that special tool I invented for cutting granite—the one you said no one would ever want because it would never work.''

''I have no recollection of any such person.''

''I'm not surprised, Bruce,'' her grandmother said tartly. ''That was the summer your father had back surgery and could have used some help getting around afterward, but you chose to remain in the city and were too busy jockeying for Head of Department status at the college, to care how we were coping. Thankfully, Matteo wasn't, and always made time to lend a hand when it was needed. I don't know how we'd have managed without him.''

Andrew, spoke up then. ''I remember him! Met him when we came out to the lake one long weekend. Nice guy, as I recall. Played a mean game of racquetball and could swim like a fish. Worked like a Trojan, too. Except when he took an hour off once in a while, I don't think I ever saw him that he wasn't up to his elbows in oil and grease, trying to get Grandfather's gadget up and running. He was a real hands-on kind of guy.''

''Now that you mention it, I remember him, too.'' Cast in his father's image, right down to the aquiline nose and prematurely iron-gray hair, Victor had curled his lip in a sneer. ''Given half a chance, he'd have had his hands all over Stephanie as well, and I don't think she'd have minded one bit.''

Stephanie had almost choked on her wine. Victor was the most self-absorbed man on the planet, yet if he'd picked up on the attraction between her and Matteo, it was more than likely that others had noticed it, too. ''That's ridiculous!''

''It had better be,'' her father ordained. ''You were taught to uphold certain standards of behavior. If I'd had any inkling that you were monkeying around with some transient laborer behind my back—!''

"Oh, Bruce, we might not have spent much time at the lake that summer, but I'm sure I'd have noticed if Stephanie did any such thing,'' her mother cut in with unusual temerity. One did not interrupt the almighty Professor Leyland when he was in full throttle; one hung on his every word and waited for permission to speak.

Just to impress on his wife how far she'd overstepped the mark, he let a second or two of thundering silence tick by before replying, "I wish I shared your certainty, Vivienne. Instead, I find myself more inclined to understand why, if sinking to the level of the lowest common denominator is what most appealed to our daughter, it's such small wonder she couldn't hold on to Charles.''

Aware that her cheeks were flaming, as much from anger as embarrassment, Stephanie had shoved back her chair and scooped Simon out of his. There was a great deal she'd have liked to say, not the least being that she'd neither submit to being reprimanded as if she were still in her teens, nor tolerate having her imperfect past served up for dessert. The days when her father's icy contempt could wound her were long gone, but she'd wait for a more propitious time to tell him so. "I think I've heard enough, and my son certainly has.''

"Touched a nerve, have we? I thought as much!''

Victor's voice had floated snidely after them as she hustled Simon inside the house, and it had taken every ounce of willpower for her not to race back to the terrace and give him a piece of her mind he wouldn't soon forget.

"Stop it this instant!'' she'd heard their grandmother snap. "Stephanie's quite right. That conversation was unfit for a child's ears, and nothing short of offensive to mine!''

So much for burying our differences, Stephanie thought

now, breathing deeply of the balmy night air and striving for a serenity that seemed bent on eluding her. Her father was as overbearing as ever, her mother as easily put in her place, and Victor as unpleasantly supercilious. Only Drew showed signs of a little humanity.

And if all that didn't present complications enough, Matteo De Luca had come back into her life, to peel away years of forgetting, and lay bare the pain of remembering how much she had loved him—and how easy it would be to fall prey to his charms a second time. Whoever had first coined the expression, *the more things change, the more they remain the same,* had known what he was talking about.

CHAPTER TWO

THOUGH small, Ischia's main town, Ischia Porto, bustled with activity. Stands of lemon trees and Indian fig separated the stretch of golden sand from expensive boutiques, hotels and beach shops. But after an hour of sight-seeing, Simon rebelled. Even watching the ferries come in to dock had lost whatever appeal it might once have held.

"I can see ferries any old time at home," he whined. "Why can't we go back to the villa and swim in the pool?"

"You can swim in a pool at home any old time, too," Stephanie pointed out, striving for patience, "but you can't explore Italy whenever the mood takes you. Come on, Simon, this is a real adventure. Just think of everything you'll be able to tell your friends about, when you get home."

"Nobody cares about a bunch of shops and old buildings, Mom! They're boring." Cheeks flushed from the heat, he trailed disconsolately beside her along the *Corso Vittoria Colonna.* "Italy's boring, as well."

From his point of view, she supposed it was. To minimize the risk of running into Matteo again, she'd dragged the boy from one village to the next over the last four days, and it was frankly too much for him. He was only just nine—not exactly of an age to appreciate spectacular scenery, or the history of an island which dated back to the eighth century B.C. But she could hardly explain her real reasons for avoiding the villa.

"Would an ice cream sundae make you feel better?" she coaxed, steering him to a table at a sidewalk café.

He shrugged and slouched onto the nearest chair. "I guess."

She ordered *Gelato Cassata* for him, the tiramisu flavor for herself, then took a tourist map from her bag and spread the sheet flat on the table. Surely she could find *something* to appeal to a boy his age! "How about a ride in a horse-drawn carriage this afternoon? That'd be fun, wouldn't it?"

"I guess." About as impressed as if she'd suggested they run behind the horse, with a shovel and pail in hand, Simon scowled and began idly kicking his foot against the base of the table. *Thud…thud…thud….*

"What about a boat trip, then?"

"If you want." *Thud…thud…thud….*

The little vase of flowers on the table wobbled precariously. Steadying it, Stephanie said, "Please stop doing that, Simon!"

He regarded her apathetically. "Doing what?"

"Kicking the table. It's irritating, and you're going to knock over these flowers. Eat your ice cream, instead."

He stared mutinously at the gelato rapidly melting in its glass dish. "I don't like it. It's got bits of stuff in it."

"They're just little pieces of candied fruit."

He poked his spoon around in the mess, sampled a tiny mouthful, and made a face. A moment later, the rhythmic thud…thud…thud…started again.

"I told you not to do that!" she said, annoyance lending a sharp edge to her voice.

He looked up, startled by her tone. "Didn't mean to, Mom," he mumbled. "Sorry."

She watched him a moment, knowing she was to blame for the misery she saw on his face. She never should have agreed to a holiday which had "disaster" stamped all over it, even before she knew Matteo De Luca was part of the mix.

"I'm doing my best here, Simon," she said at last. "Do you think you could help me out by trying to be a bit more enthusiastic?"

"I guess," he said for the third time, sounding more morose than ever.

Burying a frustrated sigh, she studied the map of the island more closely. Left to her own devices, she'd have headed west along the coast as far as the village of *Lacco Ameno,* and spent the afternoon browsing through its two museums, but she could well imagine Simon's reaction to such a suggestion. Conversely, he might possibly be interested in the thermal baths also found there, but she wasn't having her precious child cavorting in waters reputed to be the most radioactive in Italy.

She wasn't sure exactly when she became aware that she and Simon were being observed. All she knew was that, out of the blue and despite the cloying heat, a shiver passed over her skin. Slowly, with an almost preternatural sense of inevitability, she lifted her head. Her gaze immediately collided with that of the man standing across the street beside a small Fiat.

If she'd had her wits about her, she'd have grabbed Simon by the hand and run in the other direction. Instead, she sat frozen in the chair, a classic example of a deer caught in the headlights, and watched helplessly as Matteo De Luca wove a lazy path through the crowd of pedestrians, and came to a stop at her side.

Struggling to hide her dismay, she said, "Just how long have you been watching us?"

"A minute or two only. I wasn't at first sure that it was you."

"And now that you know your eyes weren't deceiving you?"

"Then I take the opportunity to say hello." With impeccable courtesy, he shook Simon's hand. "*Buon giorno,*

Signor. I'm Matteo and you, I think, must be Simon. You're enjoying your visit to Ischia?"

"No," Simon said forthrightly.

Matteo laughed and slid, uninvited, into the empty chair next to Stephanie's. "I like a boy who knows his own mind. So, what's brought you here today?"

"We're tourists," she croaked, so agitated by his nearness that she hardly knew what she was saying. "What do you think brought us here? We've come to see the sights."

Fleetingly, his gaze returned to Simon slumped miserably over his ice cream dish, before it zeroed in on her again. "Yet it appears that neither of you is having a good time."

"Appearances can be deceiving," she said, desperately trying to wrestle her thoughts into something resembling coherent order. "We're merely trying to decide where to go next."

"Don't you know that the only way to find the very best places is to turn to a local tour guide?"

"We have a very good map, thank you. We don't need a guide."

"But of course you do, *la mia bella!* Shops such as the ones you see here...." He snapped his fingers contemptuously. "They're impossible to miss and are of the kind found all over Italy. But you need someone who's familiar with every inch of this special island, to show you where knights used to fight battles and keep prisoners in dungeons." He slewed a conspiratorial glance at Simon who was now eyeing him with horrifying interest. "You'd like to visit a castle, *Signor?*"

"For real?"

"*Sì, Signor!* For very real!"

"Oh, boy!" Simon turned to Stephanie, delight transforming his features. "Can we, Mom?"

Her stomach rose up and bumped against her heart. *Sight-seeing with her son's biological father? Not likely!* "I don't think so, sweetie. I'm sure *Signor* De Luca has more important things to do."

"Not so," Matteo said, with maddening good cheer. "*Signor* De Luca took care of all his errands earlier, and has the rest of the day free."

About to refuse the offer again, this time more crushingly, Stephanie caught the changing emotions chasing over Simon's face—fledgling hope and earnest pleading, warring with tearful disappointment—and hadn't the heart to go through with it. What harm could it do, after all, to accept Matteo's offer? Exploring a castle hardly constituted a threat to a secret no one but she knew existed.

"Well," she said, blowing out another sigh, this time of defeat, "perhaps for an hour or so, but only if you're sure we're not imposing."

"I'm very sure," Matteo said, sounding so annoyingly machismo and, at the same time, looking so utterly, romantically Italian that she could barely stand it. "It'll be my very great pleasure to make your afternoon memorable in every way."

She groaned inwardly, quite certain that he'd succeed far beyond anything he realized, and chanced another look at him. Today he wore navy trousers, tailored to fit him like a glove, and highly polished black shoes. As for his shirt...!

Swallowing, she dragged her gaze away. Did his shirt have to be so blindingly white that, in contrast, his skin glowed like beaten bronze? Couldn't he have done something with his hair so that it didn't gleam black as midnight satin? And by what right did he flaunt lashes so long and thick that it was a miracle he was able to hold his eyelids open? If he was determined to insinuate himself into her afternoon, couldn't he at least have looked too ordinary to merit notice, instead of standing out in the crowd, a god among men?

"Well, Stephanie, do we have a deal?"

Left with little choice but to accept the situation as gracefully as possible, she nodded. "We have a deal."

"*Buono!* I'll find a taxi while you finish your *gelato.*"

"Taxi?" She glanced at the Fiat still parked across the street. "Isn't that your car?"

The hint of a smile crossed his face. "No, Stephanie. I didn't drive here today. I came by boat."

"All the way from Saint Angelo by ferry, you mean? I wish I'd thought of that. The people who own our villa very kindly left their Porsche for us to use, but it seats only four, so Simon and I have been taking the bus every day, and he's becoming a bit tired of it."

Matteo pressed his lips together more firmly, as if trying to prevent the smile from erupting into a full-blown grin.

Immediately suspicious, she said, "What's so funny about that?"

"Not a thing," he murmured lightly. "You make me smile, that's all."

"Why?"

"Because while others might look at you and see a woman of great beauty and sophistication, I'm reminded of a long-ago summer and a girl full of innocence and laughter."

Laughter for a little while, perhaps, she thought bitterly, *but for me, it was followed by an endless winter of tears!* "Don't make the mistake of thinking I'm still that girl fresh out of high school, too dim-witted to find her way out of a brown paper bag without help, Matteo."

His amusement abruptly vanished. "I never envisioned you as such. And if you believe that I did," he finished cryptically, "then you have even more to learn about me that I originally thought."

If that wasn't warning enough that she'd taken on more than she could handle, what followed soon after certainly brought the message home. Not that Matteo forced himself on her in any way. If anything, he treated her with casual courtesy much of the time, and chose instead to direct most of his interest, not to mention his considerable charm, on her son. And she, contrary fool that she was, smarted at being relegated to second billing.

"I will help you to speak Italian," he told Simon, when they were all three jammed in the back seat of a small taxi like so many incestuous sardines, and proceeded to devote the entire journey to teaching him simple phrases, so that he could practice them on the pretty waitress who took their pizza order when they stopped for lunch at a small waterfront *trattoria* in Ischia Ponte.

Simon proved to be an excellent student. "*Grazie,*" he said, when she set a tall glass of fruit juice before him.

She flashed him a wide smile. "*Prego, le mio piccolo signor!*"

"I think she knew what I said!" he whispered proudly, after she left to wait on another table.

"I think she's fallen in love with your handsome blue eyes, *Signor* Simon," Matteo teased.

But it seemed glaringly obvious to Stephanie that if the woman was smitten with anything, it was Matteo's dark, sultry gaze. It was enough to give a person indigestion, she thought sourly, eyeing the anchovies on her slice of pizza with acute disfavor.

Then, suddenly, he directed his thousand watt smile her way, and her irritation melted in its warmth. At twenty-five he'd been beautiful enough, but in the way that young men of that age are, before life has left its defining mark on them. At thirty-five, he was so much more than merely handsome, and she found herself fascinated beyond reason by him…left with no sense of survival…drawn by an indefinable magnetism—all that hooey she thought she'd outgrown years before.

She'd been such an awkward, love-struck adolescent! If he'd told her then to go jump into the frigid waters of Bramley Lake in winter, she would have done so without regard for the fact that she'd have been taking her life in her hands. Instead, he'd crooked his little finger, and she'd tumbled into bed—and into love—with him, in the middle of summer, and the results had been almost as disastrous.

Surely she wasn't about to make the same mistake again?

"You're looking very somber, Stephanie," Matteo remarked, studying her as she sipped her iced *caffe latte*. "Aren't you the smallest bit pleased to see me again?"

Simon had left the table and wandered down to the quayside where fishermen were hauling ashore the day's catch. "I'm keeping an eye on Simon," she said, glad of an excuse to avoid answering his question directly. "I don't want him wandering too close to the edge of the dock."

But mentioning her son was a mistake. Following her gaze, Matteo studied Simon long and hard, and Stephanie felt the fear pushing against her ribs, crowding her lungs.

What did he see? What was he thinking? Had something about Simon triggered suspicion in his mind, so that he'd begun to connect the dots?

"He's a fine looking boy, Stephanie." The observation cut across her line of thought like a hot knife through butter. "Big for his age, too. He can't be more than… what, eight?"

"He takes after his father," she said, averting her gaze and shamelessly opting for distorted truth. "Charles was a big man."

"*Was?*"

"He died not long after we divorced."

"I'm sorry. I had no idea. That must be very hard on Simon."

"He was too young at the time for it to have much effect on him." Not bothering to add how often Simon wished aloud that he had a father like other children his age, she pushed away from the table. "I think we should tour that castle now, before Simon grows restless."

"*Sono pronto*—I'm ready when you are." He called to Simon and led them to the causeway connecting the village to the rocky island from which the forbidding walls of the *Castello Aragonese* rose up. "So, which of us can run faster?" he asked, the laughter in his voice a direct challenge Simon couldn't resist, and in seconds they were off, racing each other along the narrow path.

Her disquiet increasing with every step, Stephanie followed, helpless to halt events set in motion by her own stupidity. She heard Simon's gales of laughter floating on the breeze, watched him gaze worshipfully at this new and exciting male presence who'd suddenly come into his life.

Shading her eyes from the sun, she saw the silhouette of their two figures etched against the cloudless sky: the man, so broad and tall, holding her son's—*his* son's!—hand, worming his way into the child's trusting heart, and it was as if she were imprisoned in a soundproof bubble from which there was no escape.

Be on your guard, Simon! she wanted to call out. *Don't let yourself adore him. He can't be a part of your life, no matter how badly you want him to be!* But the words bounced around in her head, sounding an urgent warning only she could hear.

"Mom?" Simon came dashing back to her, cheeks rosy with excitement, dark blond hair tousled by the breeze.

"Hurry *up!* We're waiting to go in the castle. Matteo says they used to keep people chained up in the dungeons for years. He says there's secret passages—"

"There *are* secret passages, Simon."

The point of her comment sailed blithely over his head. "How did you know? Oh, I guess Matteo told you, right? He knows *everything!*"

Hardly! she thought, rolling her eyes in despair.

"Hey, and guess what else! Matteo says there's a room where they used to put dead people on chairs and just leave them there to rot. Gross, huh?" He tugged at her hand, forcing her to pick up the pace. "Come *on,* Mom! This is going to be *so cool!*"

"Why the solemn face, Stephanie?" Matteo inquired, as she drew level with him, and Simon, bursting with impatience, went charging ahead. "You're not looking forward to touring the *Castello?*"

"If you must know, I'm not looking forward to being woken by my son's bad dreams tonight, when the horror stories you've been filling his head with come back to haunt him. What are you thinking of, frightening a child his age with stories of dead people left sitting in chairs?"

For several seconds, he subjected her to such a direct stare that she squirmed inside. Finally, he said, "If anyone is afraid, Stephanie, it's you. Your boy is having the time of his life, and the more he shows his enjoyment, the more you show your fear—of me! Care to tell me why I disturb you so deeply?"

"You don't."

"Ah, Stephanie! Many things about you might have changed. The lovely girl I once knew has grown up. Her clothes, her jewelry, her haircut, her cool reserve, all attest to a level of sophistication that young creature couldn't begin to emulate. But one thing about you remains the same. You still haven't learned how to tell a lie."

Much he knew! "And you're as shallow now as you were then. You know nothing about me except for what you see."

"Precisely." He wound a strand of her hair around his finger, just firmly enough to hold her prisoner. "Less than half an hour ago, I sat across from a woman who ought to have been perfectly at ease in that unpretentious little *trattoria* where we stopped for lunch. Yet she was nervous as a cat dancing on broken glass. She could barely force a sliver of pizza down her throat. Her eyes darted frantically from her son to me, as if she thought I might abduct him right from under her very elegant nose. The pulse at her throat beat more furiously than a hummingbird's wings. She clutched her coffee cup as if it were all that stood between her and death. Every time her son's face came alive with laughter, she winced as if he'd struck her. Those were the things I saw, *cara,* and I see them still."

Perspiration beaded her forehead; trickled between her breasts. "You have a very vivid imagination, I'll grant you that."

"Not imagination. I speak the truth, just as I always have with you. You don't trust me, and I'm at a loss to understand why." He cupped her jaw, his touch warm and firm. "Surely, after all these years, it could not be because I ended our affair?"

She felt the heat rising to her face and tried to twist free of his hold, but he refused to let her go. "That's it!" he exclaimed softly, his gaze probing the depths of her soul. "Because I hurt you once, you think I might do so again."

"Rubbish! You did me a favor, and if I didn't see that at the time, I certainly came to appreciate it later. You freed me to go on and make something of my life. So at the risk of denting your colossal ego, I'm neither afraid nor distrustful of you, Matteo. I'm simply grateful. In hindsight, you turned out to be more a friend than I gave you credit for.''

''Then prove it.''

''How?''

''Allow this friend to take you out to dinner tonight. Give me the chance to redeem myself for the cavalier way I treated you then, by showing you the kind of man I am today. Let me try to explain why I acted as I did.''

His voice, sort of velvet, sort of not, stroked past her ear and created havoc in her midsection. Smothered her in nostalgia. Made her want to recapture all the fire and passion that once had flared between them.

But she was no longer nineteen. She knew that such intense heat soon burned itself out. ''Who you are today is scarcely relevant, Matteo,'' she said, pushing his hand away and putting some distance between them. ''Nor do I see any point in rehashing the past.''

''Even if doing so clears the way for better understanding in the future?''

''We have no future,'' she said flatly, and that much, at least, was true. Because of him, she'd built the present on lies from her past; she wouldn't allow him to compromise her future in the same way.

''Perhaps not in the long term, but you're here for the rest of the month. Even if we weren't living next door to one another, the odds are high that, on an island as small as this, we'd meet time and again. Do you really want every chance encounter to be filled with such tension that you spend half your days looking over your shoulder in an effort to avoid me?''

''Frankly, no.''

''Then let us hammer out a truce in a neutral setting. Come on, Stephanie,'' he coaxed, when still she hesitated. ''What do you have to lose? I'm not asking for your firstborn, just a quiet dinner between friends, with no hidden agenda, no ulterior motive.''

His off-hand remark about laying claim to her firstborn was but one of many reasons to turn down his invitation. Yet refusing such a reasonable request merely gave credence to his allegation that she was afraid of him. Wouldn't it be better to defuse such a claim by accepting? After all, she was a lifetime older and wiser than she'd been when first they met. Harder to impress, tougher to fool. She wouldn't make the same mistakes with him again. Would she?

''Since you put it like that, why not?'' she said, with what she prayed was a carelessly indifferent shrug. ''You're absolutely right. I've got nothing to lose.''

''*Eccellente!* I'll pick you up at the villa at eight.''

''It's better if I meet you outside the gates.''

''As you wish, Stephanie,'' he said, his smile at once ironic and amused. ''You may count on me to be very discreet.''

Candlelight became her, shifting over her face and shading her eyes with mystery at the same time that it showcased her smile. Glad he'd chosen to wine and dine her in the subdued opulence of *Circolo Alongi,* a private supper club housed in a nineteenth century villa tucked high on the slopes of Mount Epomeo, he leaned back in his chair and examined her at leisure.

The setting might have been created just for her. Even as a teenager in shorts or blue jeans, she'd possessed the bearing of a princess. Here, in a dress the color of sunrise and with her blond hair swept up in a shining coil on top of her head and sparkling crystal prisms dangling from her ears, she could have been a queen. The backdrop of rich cream walls hung with fine paintings, jewel-toned silk rugs on pale marble floors, and exquisite floral arrangements on linen-covered tables, simply enhanced her love-liness.

Regarding him over the rim of her wineglass, she said, "You're staring, Matteo."

"I can't help myself. You draw the eye of every man in the room."

"Why? Have I committed some dreadful *faux pas?*"

"Not you," he replied. "I'm the only one prone to such behavior."

"By inviting me to dinner?"

He shook his head, momentarily overcome with a surge of regret so intense that it took his breath away. "I'm at a loss, Stephanie. I don't know whether to apologize to you for the way I behaved ten years ago, or thank you for making that summer the most pleasurable of my life."

She fluttered her lashes, less, he suspected, to be coy, than because she was embarrassed. A faint blush colored her skin. "We don't have to talk about it. It all happened a long time ago. You yourself said, just this afternoon, that we're not the same people we were then."

"I said *I* was not the same. But you...I don't know that you're so very different, after all. I see many traces of that long-ago girl in the woman you've become, many of her traits. But at twenty-five, I was arrogant, selfish, and too immature to appreciate your fine qualities. I seduced you, put your good name in jeopardy, and left you to face the consequences alone. And I'm proud of none of it."

"There were no consequences," she said, her blush deepening, "and you ought to know."

"I don't wish to be indelicate," he was quick to reply, "nor have I any desire to revive unpleasant memories, but just because I used protection to guard against your becoming pregnant doesn't alter the fact that, in every other respect, I treated you shabbily."

"You were honest, Matteo."

"Brutal, I'd say."

"All right, brutally honest, then! What I saw as love everlasting, you recognized as infatuation. And a good thing, too! We were mismatched from the start." She toyed with her Veal Frangelico and ventured a smile. "Can you really see me married to someone like you?"

"The princess and the pauper, you mean?"

"Not necessarily. But we came from vastly different worlds and had little in common beyond an overabundance of hormones. Without meaning to offend you at all, I feel bound to say that if you hadn't ended our affair, I would have—and sooner rather than later. Let's face it, Matteo: we were wrong for each other from the outset."

"And you were looking for *Signor* Right."

She turned to stare out the window at the lights of Saint Angelo spattered over the shoreline far below. "Yes."

"And you found him soon after I vacated the scene." He took a mouthful of wine, and wondered why the smooth, robust Bertillon should all at once leave such a harsh impression on his palate. "Tell me about this man you married."

"There's little to tell. We were together for only two years."

"So he wasn't *Signor* Right, after all."

"I thought he was, at the time. I thought he loved me."

"And you loved him?"

A spark of something darkened her eyes, like a coming storm threatening a clear blue sky, and she took a moment to reply. "I told myself I did. It's easy to convince yourself of that, when your entire family approves."

"Is that why you rushed into marriage? To please your family?"

"No. Charles and I reached that decision together. I was ready to settle down."

"Ready for a child, too?"

She cast her eyes down and stared at her lap. "Yes. Charles wanted the baby. He was quite a bit older than I was, you see."

Not exactly! As far as Matteo knew, a man's age had little to do with his ability to father a child. But she seemed distracted by the turn the conversation had taken, so he endeavored to end it on a more positive note. "At least you were happy for a little while."

"I've been happy for a long while, Matteo," she informed him sharply. "My life is very full and satisfying. I have Simon, and a very rewarding career—"

"What career is that?"

"I'm a microbiologist, working in a research facility at the university. I thought you'd have known that, since you've always kept in touch with my grandmother."

He didn't tell her that, once he heard she was married, he'd found her too painful a topic to pursue. Instead, he said mildly enough, "And those two things are enough?"

"Oh, there's more," she said cheerfully.

Too cheerfully for his liking! No doubt there was also a lineup of eligible bachelors dancing attendance on her during her leisure hours—perhaps even a special man wanting to make her his wife, a possibility that, oddly, left him black with suppressed rage. "Such as what?"

"I have a beautiful home in a beautiful city. Friends, enough money, good health, peace of mind...what more could I ask for?"

"Love?"

"I already told you, I have Simon."

"Not that kind of love, Stephanie. Some women don't need passion to make them complete, but you're not one of them. You were made to be loved by a man."

"I don't have time for romance, or marriage. I'm too busy being a mother. And men usually aren't willing to take on another man's child."

Masking his relief, he said, "I don't see why not, when the child in question is so thoroughly likeable—lovable, even."

She bit her lip, and in doing so drew his attention to her mouth. As if it had last happened just yesterday, he recalled how it had felt to kiss her, and the embers which had been simmering low in his belly almost from the moment he saw her again, burst into flame.

Quickly, before she guessed the direction of his thoughts, he said, "And a boy needs a father figure in his life, you know. Someone to give him proper guidance."

He meant well by his words, but she didn't receive them in the same spirit. "Does he really?" she snapped, her hands suddenly shaking so hard that her knife and fork fell with a clatter onto her plate. "Well, thank you so much for your expert advice, but it just so happens that Simon is managing very well with just his mother's guidance."

He raised his hands in surrender. "I'm sorry if I've offended you. It—"

"Oh, save it for someone who cares, Matteo!" Visibly distraught, she pushed back her chair and sprang away from the table. "This evening was a mistake. I knew before it even started that I'd live to regret it."

"Stephanie, wait!" he exclaimed, stunned by her outburst.

But he found himself addressing thin air. In a swirl of rosy silk, she was gone, running from the dining room as if the hounds of hell were nipping at her heels. Flinging down his napkin, he went in pursuit and almost caught up with her. But she reached the ladies' room just in time to slip through the door and slam it in his face.

Chagrined, he turned away and met the amused gaze of Luigi, the club's head steward. The man lifted his shoulders in a shrug, as though to say, *Women! How is a man to understand the workings of their minds!*

Right there and then, Matteo had no answer. Where Stephanie was concerned, however, he intended to figure one out. Because while he might have relegated her to the back of his mind for years, ever since she'd come into his life again, she was *all* he'd been able to think about, and he wanted to know everything about her.

Most particularly, he wanted to know why she was so afraid of him. Why, when he was trying his best to prove himself worthy of her friendship, she persisted in regarding him as the enemy.

CHAPTER THREE

EVERYONE was in bed when Stephanie returned to the villa shortly before midnight. Carrying her shoes, she crept up the stairs and peeped in on Simon. He slept like an angel, blissfully ignorant of how close his mother had come to turning his world upside-down.

"I was beginning to think you planned to spend the night in there," Matteo had said, waylaying her when she finally left the sanctuary of the ladies' room at the supper club. "Stephanie, forgive me for upsetting you. That wasn't my intention. I intended no criticism."

Doing her best to hide how shaken she'd been by his comments, she'd managed a smile. "It wasn't entirely your fault. I'm afraid I overreacted. Mothers, especially single mothers, tend to do that when they feel they're under attack from an outsider."

His dark, level brows rose. "An outsider?" he said, sounding as wounded as if she'd stabbed him in the heart with a carving knife. "What, have I so soon lost the right to consider myself your friend?"

"Perhaps we were expecting too much in thinking friendship between us was possible."

"Not so!" He caught both her hands in his. "I have nothing but admiration for you, both as a woman and a mother, and the last thing I'd ever want is to cause you pain. If you believe nothing else I tell you, I beg you to believe that."

Unfortunately, she did. He *wasn't* the same man who'd stolen her heart, along with her innocence. There was a humanity and compassion to him now which he hadn't possessed before. Yet he was no less alluring. Not only had maturity softened his arrogance, it also added to his sex appeal, which made him all the more dangerous.

It would be easy to fall under his spell again; to lower her guard and leave herself vulnerable to his insidious charm. Look at what had happened tonight: his smile across a candlelit table, a glass or two of wine, and the next thing she knew, she was betraying damaging evidence that she wasn't nearly as immune to him as she'd like him and her both to believe. Even the simple *friendly* way he now clasped her hands was enough to send tendrils of heat curling through her blood, and leave her hungering for more.

"I'll consider the matter," she said, pulling herself free and deliberately keeping her tone light. "Right now, though, I'd like you to take me home."

"So soon? Can't I persuade you to share coffee and an after-dinner *grappa* with me, first?"

"I have the feeling I should pass. I'm not sure what *grappa* is, but it sounds sinful."

"It's nothing but an Italian brandy made from the stalks of grapes. Harmless enough when taken in moderation, and a pleasant way to end the evening." Cupping her elbow, he ushered her toward a wide marble staircase. "And a little sin once in a while never hurt anyone."

He made sin sound delectable. Something worth dying for! He always had. And she'd never been able to resist it. "But it's growing late," she said, a token, feeble objection at best.

He laughed. "It's not quite ten o'clock, Stephanie— barely the dinner hour in this part of the world!"

"Nevertheless, it's past my bedtime."

"I'd have thought you were also past the age where

you had to obey a curfew. Surely your father won't be waiting up to see what time you get home?''

"No. My parents and brothers drove into Forio for dinner, but I begged off going with them. Only my grandmother knows I'm out with you. She offered to look after Simon.''

"I see." His lashes swept down, concealing the expression in his eyes. "Still afraid the rest of your family won't approve of the company you're keeping, then?"

"You're not the only one who's different, Matteo," she informed him tartly. "Despite what you might think, I've grown up, too. My life's my own now. I do as I please, and spend time with whomever I please. But I saw no point in inviting unnecessary comment by making a big issue of having dinner with you."

"Then don't make a big issue of finishing the evening in style, with coffee and brandy." He smiled and let his eyes sweep the length of her. "You can hardly blame me for wanting to show you off, *cara*. It's not every night that I have such a beautiful woman on my arm."

That smile, coupled with his lazy, heavily-lashed glance, laid waste to a woman's intentions and left her sense of self-preservation in ruins. Bemused, Stephanie allowed him to lead her up the stairs to a lounge softly lit by crystal chandeliers, and elegantly furnished with deep, comfortable couches upholstered in silk tapestry.

After a brief exchange with a hovering waiter, Matteo led her to a quiet alcove separated from the rest of the room by a lacquered screen. They were barely seated before the same waiter reappeared, rolling before him a small brass trolley set with a silver coffeepot, translucent porcelain *demi tasses* rimmed in burgundy and gold, a decanter of what she presumed was the *grappa*, and two tall, narrow glasses similar to champagne flutes, but flared at the lip like bud vases.

"I chose the *Aglianico* for your introduction to our brandy," Matteo said, pouring a measure of the liquor into each glass and passing one to her. "It possesses the floral notes of an orchard which I think you'll enjoy. *Salute!*"

Cautiously, she tasted the contents, and choked as the liquid seared her throat and left her fighting for breath. "You could have warned me I was playing with fire!" she gasped, when she could speak again.

"But it is a fire you can tame, Stephanie. Take but a small amount, the next time. Let it linger on your palate...caress your tongue."

Out of the blue, the hypnotic cadence of his voice drew her back with shocking recall to the first time he'd kissed her. *Open your mouth, Stephanie...let me taste you....*

Appalled by the telltale quiver of sexual arousal spearing the length of her, she lifted the glass to her lips a second time, not caring if she burned a hole in her throat. Anything to silence the seductive memories of yesterday!

"Slowly, *cara*," he purred. "Ah yes...just so! Now hold it a moment before you release it. Close your eyes, and let it stroke your senses."

She had no intention of doing any such thing. However, his powers of persuasion far exceeded her puny efforts at resistance and, astonishingly, her eyelids fluttered closed, shutting out the subdued light of the chandeliers. But not, alas, the images surging up from the past and swimming through her mind in living color.

She saw again the stable loft, and the halo of yellow light cast on the hay by the lantern hanging from a beam. Saw him stripped naked, his skin olive-tinted from hip to mid-thigh, but elsewhere burnished by the sun. Saw him stretched out beside her. Felt him draw her hand inexorably toward him until the dark hair at his groin feathered against her skin, and the powerful thrust of his erection nudged at her fingertips.

Once again, his whispered entreaty drifted down the years, hoarse and impassioned. *"Touch me, Stephanie… feel me…stroke me…."*

Eyes flying wide open, she sampled the *grappa* again with reckless abandon. Let the blasted stuff choke the life out of her, if it chose! At least that would put paid to ill-timed, inappropriate memories sneaking up and engulfing her without warning.

But this time, the brandy rolled down her throat, smooth as a skein of silken ribbon. It wound its way past the constriction in her chest, warming her blood to the tips of her toes. And opening the door to the past even wider.

From the outset, Matteo had beguiled her with his dazzling, devil-may-care grin and midnight-dark, seductive bedroom eyes. He was a rebel who loved danger and thumbed his nose at the conservative world in which she'd grown up, and if one part of her had known he was bad for her and would bring her nothing but grief, another was drawn to his wild and reckless ways as inexorably as a moth to the flame.

One afternoon in particular stood out in her memory, when he'd lured her up to the hayloft, and right in the middle of their making love, her grandfather had come into the stable. She'd frozen, aghast at being discovered, and attempted to roll free. But Matteo had pinned her with his body and shaken his head in refusal. He'd smiled into her eyes and rocked silently within her, teasing her flesh unbearably.

She'd tried to distance herself emotionally, physically, but danger seemed to heighten her body's sexual appetite. Despite all her efforts, she'd felt herself teetering on the brink of orgasm. Had been sure her thundering heart could be heard a mile away. And when she finally succumbed to the explosive release, he'd covered her mouth with his hand to stifle her involuntary moans of pleasure.

"Well, Stephanie?"

Focusing her gaze with difficulty, she saw Matteo watching her. "Well, what?"

"I asked if you'd care for more *grappa.*"

Absolutely not! She wasn't much of a drinker at the best of times, and this concoction was lethal! It diminished her common sense and made flirting with danger too appealing. On the plus side, though, the warmth of the liquor had a relaxing effect, left her feeling less brittle, less edgy. "Well...maybe just a splash. It's very potent."

"*Sì.* The first time can be something of a shock to someone not used to it. But it improves upon acquaintance, does it not?"

"*Did I hurt you, my Stephanie?*" he'd murmured, the night she'd lost her virginity to him. "*I'm sorry. It will be better the next time, I promise...you will come also, and it will be beautiful for both of us....*"

"And it was!"

"*Scusi?*" Matteo had leaned forward on the couch and was staring at her, his eyes watchful, his brow knit with confusion.

She grasped at the edges of the memories confounding her, ineffectually trying to contain them, but they slithered, sharp and brilliant, through her mind—of his mouth at her breast, and his hand delving between her legs. Of him looming tall and strong above her, and the stabbing discomfort as he entered her, followed by the engulfing heat of his possession. Of her own whimper of pain, drowned out by his deep groan of completion.

"It *does,*" she stammered. "Improve upon acquaintance, that is. The *grappa,* I mean...."

"Of course." He lifted the coffeepot. "And marries well with espresso."

She heard the lazy laughter in his voice and knew he must find her a joke. Small wonder! She was acting like a perfect idiot.

"So," he said, sinking back next to her on the couch after the coffee was poured, "how are you enjoying the *Villa Elenna?*"

"Very much. It's quite lovely inside. Have you ever seen it?"

A smile played over his mouth. "A few times, yes. It is, as you say, quite lovely."

The coffee was too hot to drink. Setting it aside, she sipped again from her glass. "What's your cottage like, Matteo?"

"Very comfortable. I'll be happy to show it to you sometime, if you like."

The mere idea sent an illicit shiver of pleasure over her. Ignoring it, she said primly, "You live alone, do you?"

"*Sì.*"

"Have you never been tempted to marry?"

"No."

"Don't you ever get lonely?"

He inspected his glass, held negligently between his fingers. When he looked up again, she saw his dark eyes still danced with amusement. "Just because a man is single and chooses to live alone doesn't necessarily mean he's without companionship, *cara.*"

"Well, of course it doesn't!" she said, stung. Not for a moment had she thought he'd given up women, just because he'd grown tired of her! "How naive do you think I am?"

"Quite a lot more than you'd like me to believe," he said with unflinching candor. "You are, by nature, without guile. Everything you feel is laid out for the rest of the world to see—and to trample on, should it feel so inclined."

She raised her glass again, took another mouthful of the *grappa,* and savored it as he'd instructed her to do, before allowing it to slide down her throat. "You think you know me so well, Matteo," she told him, her tongue finding its way with difficulty around her words as the warmth of the liquor ran through her blood, "but the fact of the matter is, you couldn't be farther off the mark."

"I know you're easily crushed, and very vulnerable to rejection. I rather think that's why, so soon after I left you, you married a man old enough to be your father. Because he represented safety and stability and constancy. All those things which, at the time, I couldn't—or wouldn't—give you."

"If it makes you feel better to believe that, go right ahead."

Oh dear! Had she slurred her reply a little? Turned "makes" into "makesh"?

But if Matteo noticed she'd had a little trouble articulating clearly, he gave no indication. "How did you meet him, anyway, this short-term late husband of yours? You always said you planned to attend the college where your father teaches."

"I changed my mind and moved to the west coast. Charles was one of my university profs."

"Wasn't it professionally unethical for a man in his position to become romantically involved with one of his students?"

"You're a fine one to talk about ethics!" she snorted, downing another sip of brandy. "At least he had the decency to stand by me when he found out about the...."

Oh, good grief, that tore it! Aghast at what she'd almost let slip, she shrank against the back of the couch and clamped her lips together.

"Do go on," Matteo prompted gently. "When he found about what, Stephanie?"

If, a moment before, she'd felt a pleasant buzz from the brandy, it very quickly evaporated and left her horribly clear-headed. Marshaling her thoughts and all too aware that she'd painted herself into an impossible corner, she decided brazen nerve offered the only avenue of escape.

"When he found out we were expecting a baby, Matteo. Yes, we had to get married, as they used to say in the old days."

"I see."

"Well, don't look so shocked! It happens to the best of couples. And after all, you were the one who introduced me to the joys of sex, so you shouldn't be too surprised that I developed quite a taste for it."

"As you appear to have for *grappa*," he said grimly, moving her glass out of reach. "Keep your voice down, *cara*. There's no need to inform the whole room of your adolescent exploits."

She peeped around the lacquered screen, saw the heads of other guests turned her way, and wanted to die. But she'd weathered worse humiliation, and she'd survive this.

Drawing the tattered threads of her dignity around her, she looked him straight in the eye and said stiffly, "You're quite right, Matteo. I'm afraid the brandy's gone to my head. I've made an utter fool of myself, and offended you into the bargain."

"Don't concern yourself about me. I have broad shoulders. But your husband…!" He made a sound of disgust. "For a man his age to take such advantage of a girl—"

"It wasn't like that," she felt conscience-bound to explain. "Charles was a good man. But at the time that we met, we were both…fragile. I took it rather hard when you and I broke up. Teenagers are apt to think their lives are over when their first love comes to an end, and I was no exception."

"And what was his excuse? That he was in the throes

of a midlife crisis and looking for a child-bride to restore his youth?''

''He was a recent widower. His wife and daughter had been killed in an automobile accident just three months earlier. I suppose, if you must put a label on it, we were both on the rebound. We wanted to be close to someone again. Have someone to lean on, someone who *under-stood* our pain and made it go away. By the time we realized there aren't any shortcuts, that you can't just plug in another face and another name, and expect to cobble your life back together and make it the same as it was before, it was too late. We were married.''

''And had a son.''

''Yes,'' she said evenly. ''We had a son.''

''Who wasn't reason enough for his parents to work at saving their marriage.''

''Sometimes, Matteo,'' she said on a sigh, doing her utmost to cut through the deceit and utilize whatever grains of truth she could find, ''the *only* way to move forward is to cut your losses. That's what Charles and I did.''

''Regardless of the cost to your boy.'' He shook his head. ''I confess, I don't understand the logic of it all. Surely it's always in the best interests of a child to have both his parents in his life?''

Trying very hard to keep her voice steady, Stephanie said, ''I'm not sure what makes you such an expert on family dynamics, but this much I do know. Charles and I did not reach our decision lightly, and I do not have to justify it to you, or anyone else. Simon is a happy, well-adjusted child who knows he is dearly loved, and in the end, *that's* all that counts.'' Very deliberately, she placed her coffee cup on the trolley, picked up her purse, and rose from the couch. ''And since we're never going to see eye-to-eye on the matter, there's no point in continuing this conversation. So, if it's all the same to you, I'd like to go home now.''

"Of course,'' he said, getting to his feet also. "I can see that you're tired.''

Tired? Emotionally drained was more like it! Clinging for dear life to the marble banister, she went ahead of him down the stairs. Now that the immediate threat of exposure was past, delayed reaction set in, and she felt weak all over at the realization of how close she'd come to making a complete disaster of her and Simon's life.

She and Matteo exchanged not a word during the drive back to the villa, although she was aware that he glanced at her occasionally. But she stared straight ahead and refused to acknowledge him.

Given her way, when he drew the car up outside the *Villa Elenna*, she'd have hopped out and disappeared through the gates with no more than a cursory "good night.'' He was too quick for her, though. The vehicle had barely cruised to a stop before he was out of the driver's seat and coming around to open her door.

"Thank you,'' she said. "Dinner was excellent and I had a very nice time…for the most part.''

"Perhaps we can do it again before you leave.''

She hesitated, torn between temptation and caution. In the end, the latter won out and she turned toward the villa's big iron gates, knowing that the sooner she was safely on their other side, the better off she'd be. "Let's not push our luck, Matteo. As you must have gathered, I don't deal too well with criticism, and you don't appear willing to keep your unwelcome opinions to yourself.''

She had no inkling how closely he'd followed her until his breath feathered over the nape of her neck. "And if I promise to steer well clear of your past affairs, and concentrate solely on the pleasure of your company, would you then change your mind?'' he asked, resting his hands on her shoulders.

She quivered beneath his touch and he, recognizing the indecision tormenting her, tightened his hold and spun her around to face him. ''Say 'yes,' Stephanie,'' he urged.

She lifted her face, intending to fell him with a haughty stare and a second refusal. Instead, her mouth blundered against his, and she was lost.

The night turned black, but inside her head a thousand brilliant falling stars exploded. Helplessly, she clutched at him. Dug her nails into the swell of muscle at his shoulders and prayed for deliverance from the melting hunger assailing her.

His hands slid to her waist and pulled her hard against him.

''Say 'yes,' he muttered again.

''Yes,'' she whispered, so hopelessly caught up in the sheer wonder of the moment that she'd have done anything to prolong it. Feeling him pressed against her again, his mouth moving restlessly over hers, hungry, demanding, was the *only* thing that mattered. ''Yes!''

It was as if a dam burst then, sweeping aside layer after layer of hurt and resentment in a torrent of pure, cleansing emotion. All the long, empty years of lying alone in her bed, wondering if she'd ever again know the kind of soaring pleasure she'd once found with him, dispersed in the heat of his kiss like thistledown on a summer breeze.

She dared to slip her arms around his neck; to touch his hair and inhale the scent of his skin. To taste his mouth as freely as he tasted hers. To fit her body to the shape of his, limb to limb, and heart to heart.

At last, cradling her face between his hands, he stared down at her, his dark eyes glimmering in the moonlight. ''Has it really been ten years, *carissima?*'' he murmured. ''Somehow, it seems it was just yesterday that I made you mine. Can we not pick up where we left off, and see where it might lead us?''

She traced the shape of his mouth with trembling fingers, all too vibrantly cognizant of where renewed passion would lead. To greater heartbreak for her, and utter disillusionment for him. Because from everything he'd said tonight, she knew without a shadow of doubt that he'd never forgive her for having kept his son from him.

''Better not to tempt fate,'' she said, blinking away a sudden rush of tears. ''Better to leave things as they are.''

For a second, she thought he would argue the point, and braced herself to resist him. But at the last, he stepped back and let her go. ''For tonight, perhaps,'' he said. ''But I give you fair warning now, Stephanie: tomorrow is another day, and I've never been a man to concede defeat easily.''

Looking down now at her beautiful sleeping child, despair at the unkindness of fate washed over Stephanie in unrelenting waves. If she and Matteo were destined to find lasting love, why couldn't it have been *then,* when she had nothing to hide and nothing to fear, instead of *now* when so much history lay between them?

''It isn't fair!'' she mourned silently, turning away from Simon's bed, then gave a strangled gasp as her face, pale in the dim light, swam before her in the ornate gilded mirror hanging over the dresser.

No, it isn't fair. And whose fault is that, Stephanie? Who's the one who ran away because she was too cowardly to stay and face the consequences of her actions? Who cared more about what her family might think, than she did about how the father of her child might react to news of her pregnancy? her reflection inquired.

Shamefaced, she whispered, "I did."

Exactly! that remorseless other self replied. *You're the one who started the lies. Now you'll have to live with them.*

CHAPTER FOUR

THE next morning, her grandmother took Stephanie aside and said, "While you were all out last night, your grandfather and I had a visitor. The widow from next door stopped by to invite everyone over for lunch today, and I accepted. She specifically said to be sure to let you know that Simon's included."

Stephanie wished she could come up with a good reason to decline, not because she had anything against the widow next door, but because she had no wish to risk running into Matteo again. If she'd learned nothing else last night, she knew with absolute certainty that she had to keep her distance from him. He was as addictive as a narcotic, and every bit as harmful.

Noting her hesitation, her grandmother said with a wry laugh, "Corinna's a perfectly lovely woman. Your grandfather was quite smitten by her. I think you'll like her, Stephanie."

"I'm sure I will." Stephanie chewed her lip, weighing the pleasure of a social occasion at which her father and older brother would feel obligated to put on their best party manners, against the very slight chance that she might cross paths with Matteo. He rented the gardener's cottage, after all, not part of the main house, and might very well not even be on the premises that day.

"Then why the indecision? Is spending time with the rest of us so very tedious, my love?"

"No, of course not!" she said contritely, knowing full well what high hopes her grandmother had pinned on their family reunion.

"Then you'll come with us?"

"Yes. I'm looking forward to it." And she absolutely *would not* allow thoughts of Matteo to intrude and spoil the occasion.

"Wonderful! Corinna expects us at noon, and said we'll be lunching in the garden and should dress casually."

Later that morning, after spending an hour in the pool with Simon, Stephanie surveyed her wardrobe and wondered exactly what, in the widow's eyes, constituted "casual." Although shorts and halter tops were common enough among the tourists she'd seen, residents of the island, particularly older women, seemed inclined toward a more formal style of dress. That being so, she decided to err on the side of caution, and chose a navy striped dress with elbow length sleeves and a hem which just skimmed her knees, and flat navy sandals.

The rest of the family had assembled on the terrace when she came downstairs with Simon. "Well, let's get this over with," her father declared, looking much put-upon, while her mother fluttered anxiously in the background. "I hope you'll remember your manners, Simon. If there's one thing I can't abide, it's a child who misbehaves. Remember to eat with your mouth closed and keep your elbows off the table. And don't speak unless you're spoken to."

"That'll do, Bruce," Stephanie's grandfather ordered, before she could get in a word, which was just as well since those bubbling on the tip of her tongue were scarcely fit for Simon's young ears. "I think we've all seen enough of the boy this last few days to know that Stephanie's done a first-rate job of teaching him what's what."

On that congenial note, they all trooped down the steps and headed for the next door property. "This shindig had better not last all afternoon,'' Victor said dourly, as they passed under the flower-draped pergola at the fork in the path. "Lonely widows bleating on about their dead husbands aren't my idea of entertainment.''

Overhearing, his grandmother said, "You might be in for a pleasant surprise, Victor. Not everyone is as self-involved as you appear to believe.''

"Women are,'' he replied. "Why else do you suppose I've never married?''

Bringing up the rear with Simon and her mother, Stephanie said bluntly, "I can think of a few reasons, Victor, but I imagine it'd be a waste of breath trying to explain them to you, since your mind's made up and you don't care to be confounded by facts.''

Her mother let out a nervous titter, Drew buried a grin, but her father and Victor looked thoroughly outraged. Victor's failed relationships might be legendary, but it was unheard of for anyone in the family to dare suggest *he* might be more to blame than the hapless women he became involved with.

"I suppose, having managed to screw up your own marriage, that you're the voice of experience?'' he sneered.

"At least I'm not afraid to admit I made a mistake.''

"Some of us choose not to make mistakes at all, Stephanie,'' her father pronounced.

"And some of us are human,'' she retorted, ignoring his affronted glare. For heaven's sake, how old did she have to be, before he accepted that, while she'd always be his youngest offspring, she'd long since outgrown childhood? Would he ever show any respect for her opinions, or leap to her defense as he repeatedly leaped to Victor's?

Probably not, but how much did it matter after all this time? She'd made a life outside her father's sphere of influence, and as long as she had Simon, she didn't need anyone else's approval.

Comforted by the thought, she tucked her hand more firmly around her son's and, when a turn in the path brought into view a charming miniature villa fronted by a courtyard, she marched past without turning a hair. If that was where Matteo lived, he could hang from the upper balcony and yodel, if he so chose. If she could emerge unscathed from a verbal altercation with her father, she could certainly weather anything Matteo De Luca served up.

Set in manicured gardens, the main house was an architectural masterpiece of classic curves and lemon stucco walls draped in bougainvillea. A long, oval swimming pool lay at the foot of a shallow flight of steps which led up to a terrace filled with ornate wrought iron furniture, and shaded by bright orange umbrellas.

As the guests approached, a brilliantly feathered parrot hopped up and down on its perch in a bamboo cage, and screeched raucously, *"Ciao! Avanti! Avanti!"*

Right on cue, a woman emerged from the villa and came down the steps to meet them. *"Buon giorno!"* she called out in a rich, melodious voice. *"Signor e Signora* Leyland, I'm delighted you're here."

"Ciao!" the parrot squawked again, fixing Simon in a malevolent yellow stare. *"E sposato?"*

The woman laughed merrily. "No, Guido, the young *signor* is not married!"

Still eyeing Simon, Guido hopped closer to the bars of his cage and ruffled his crest in a ludicrous parody of flirtation. *"Come si chiama, innamorato?"*

"He wants to know your name, *signor*," the woman said, with a smile.

"Simon Matthew Leyland-Owen," Simon dutifully replied, at which Stephanie cringed a little. Her decision to name him after his father, and to match his initials to his parents', suddenly didn't seem such a smart idea.

If the woman picked up on the coincidence, she made no mention of it. "*Ciao,* Simon." *See-mon,* she pronounced it, drawing out the word and somehow turning it into a song. "I am *Signora* Russo, but you may call me Corinna." She squeezed both his hands, then extended a graceful arm in a gesture which embraced the rest of them. "It is my pleasure to welcome all of you to the *Villa Aurelia!*"

A flurry of introductions followed, under cover of which Stephanie hastily revised her notions of what the term "widow" meant, as it applied to their hostess. *Signora* Russo's white strapless sundress showed off an extraordinary amount of skin, all of it so evenly tanned that she might have been dipped in molten gold. Add to that, gleaming black hair swinging around her perfect shoulders, exotic topaz eyes, a wide, dazzling smile, and long, shapely legs, and the result was so far removed from the stereotypical drab Italian widow that it was laughable.

Or perhaps not, Stephanie thought with a stab of dismay, unobtrusively scrutinizing Corinna as she ushered everyone to the terrace. This stunning, sophisticated, fortyish *widow* also happened to be Matteo's employer and very close neighbor.

As if allowing him entry to her thoughts was all it took to conjure him up in the flesh, a tall—and to Stephanie at least—instantly recognizable figure materialized from inside the villa. and strolled across the terrace to greet them. Well, so much for looking the other way when she'd passed his cottage!

"*Buon giorno!*" he said, seeming so entirely comfortable in the role of host that Stephanie was instantly suspicious.

Looking good enough to eat in khaki shorts and an

open-necked short-sleeved blue shirt, he bent to kiss her grandmother's cheek. "It's been too long since I did that, *Signora* Anna," he murmured, before turning to shake Stephanie's grandfather's hand. "*Signor* Brandon, what a pleasure to find you looking so well."

"I see no introductions are necessary here," Corinna cooed, altogether too fondly for Stephanie's liking. "It has been many years perhaps since you were last together with Matteo, but I'm sure you will agree with me that he is an unforgettable acquaintance."

Acquaintance, my left foot! Stephanie thought savagely, noting the easy intimacy with which Corinna slipped her arm through Matteo's and leaned against him.

What was it he'd said last night? *Just because a man is single and chooses to live alone doesn't mean he's without companionship....* Well, if she hadn't figured out what he meant at the time, she was certainly getting the message loud and clear now!

Unaware of his sister's turmoil, Drew nodded amiably. "Nice to see you again, Matt."

"De Luca." Although he offered Matteo his hand, Stephanie's father wrinkled his nose, as if he'd just been presented with a fillet of very stale fish.

Ever the carbon copy of his father, Victor shook hands also. "Hardly expected to find you here, De Luca," he said, sounding so absurdly pompous that Stephanie would have laughed aloud if she hadn't been so mortified. "Wouldn't have thought it was your kind of party."

"Well, you know what we Italian peasants are like," Matteo drawled, giving a beaming Simon a high-five. "Any chance for a free meal, and we're the first in line."

Stephanie could have smacked him for provoking Victor to more insults, but Corinna seemed to find Matteo's reply highly entertaining. Nudging him with one bare, sun-kissed shoulder, she chirped, "*Caro*, you are such a tease! Behave and be a good host. It'll be a few minutes yet before Baptiste serves lunch, but a glass of wine would sit well in the meantime, *sì?*"

He bathed her in a slow, appreciative smile. *"Sì."*

He'd smiled at Stephanie just the same way last night— as if she were the only woman in the world, when clearly she was but one of many, and she swung her gaze aside now, unable to stomach the scene unfolding before her.

"Pour for us, then, won't you?" Corinna crooned winsomely.

From the corner of her eye, Stephanie watched as, with the alacrity of a well-trained dog, Matteo leaped to do the widow's bidding. She, meanwhile, settled on a *chaise longue* and beckoned to Simon. To Stephanie's utter disgust, he went willingly, and curled up next to her when Corinna made room for him on the *chaise*.

"So, my handsome young friend," she purred, idly stroking the hair from his forehead, "I think perhaps you're a little young for wine, but Matteo tells me you enjoy *limonata*—lemonade, you call it in Canada, yes?"

"Yes."

"And in such hot weather, you would like a glass now?"

"Yes," Simon said again, then before his grandfather could cut in with a sharp reminder, quickly added, "Please."

Sidling up to where Stephanie remained standing at the edge of the terrace with Drew, Victor inquired in a low voice, "How the devil does De Luca know what Simon likes?"

Clearly out of patience, Drew rolled his eyes. "Probably because, like me, he's yet to meet a kid who *doesn't* like lemonade. For crying out loud, Victor, stop being so almighty stiff-necked, and try giving someone the benefit of the doubt, for a change!"

After delivering that salvo of unsolicited advice, he left Stephanie to deal with the repercussions, and went to help Matteo, who was uncorking bottles of wine at an outdoor bar.

"I don't buy his line of reasoning for a minute," Victor said, staring after him. "But then, Drew's never been much of a judge of character. Take it from me, Stephanie, De Luca's a pushy opportunist, and you'd be doing yourself and that boy a favor if you were a bit more selective about the company you keep."

He continued droning on at some length, but Stephanie barely heard a word. Instead, she stood frozen at the edge of the terrace as Corinna smiled and, cupping Simon's cheek, tipped his face up to hers and studied it closely.

Finally, after several long seconds, she murmured thoughtfully, "So *biondo,* yet somehow so...*familiare*.... What is it about you, my sweet Simon Matthew, that leaves me feeling we have met before?"

At that, Stephanie's blood ran cold. She hadn't a clue what *biondo* meant, but *familiare* needed no translation, and she'd have had to be brain dead not to recognize that, although she had searched for a resemblance between Simon and Matteo and been certain she'd seen none, Corinna had unwittingly found something.

Oh, the woman had no idea the trouble she could stir up by poking her elegant nose into matters which were none of her concern!

Mind your own business, please! Stephanie tried telegraphing. But Corinna's glance shifted to Matteo, and lingered on him speculatively as he and Drew loaded a tray with long-stemmed glasses.

Stephanie tensed, appalled at what might happen next. But, shaking her head so that her glossy hair shimmied about her shoulders in sultry waves, Corinna turned her attention back to Simon and said only, "Here comes your uncle with your *limonata, mio bello ragazzo*—my beautiful boy! When you have drunk it, go sit by the fishpond, if you like, or visit my bird and butterfly garden down there beyond Guido's cage. I feel you growing restless here, keeping company with a woman so much older and duller than you are."

Older and duller? In a pig's eye! Stephanie thought numbly. Corinna gave even the incomparable Sophia Loren a run for her money!

As for the suave, sophisticated Matteo, he'd certainly come a long way from his humble beginnings. Little remained of the quarry worker she'd known, except for his simmering sex appeal, and even that had undergone subtle change. He exercised it now with a finesse which made it all the more tantalizing.

Had Corinna been his tutor?

Simon, meanwhile, seeming as glad to escape as Stephanie was to see him leave, slid off the chaise and ran off to explore the gardens. At once, Corinna became the gracious hostess again and, as Matteo began handing out glasses, said, "We are serving you *Biancolella,* one of our fine local white wines. We hope you enjoy it."

We are serving...we hope you enjoy...! Floored by the surge of jealousy unleashing its poison into her bloodstream, Stephanie accepted a glass of wine from Drew, and sank into a chair on the fringe of the crowd.

Why didn't Corinna just stick a Sold sign on Matteo's forehead, and have done with it? she wondered, sick to the stomach as she watched the woman incline her dark, glossy head to his, and lay a possessive hand against his chest. Why bother perpetuating the myth that he lived in the gardener's cottage, when Stephanie would have bet money on it that he spent most nights in the widow's bed?

"There's something unpleasant in your glass, Stephanie? A fly, perhaps?"

Buried in her own private world of misery, she didn't realize Matteo had approached until he spoke. "No," she said, realizing he'd positioned himself so that his body acted as privacy screen between her and the rest of the party. "Why would you think such a thing?"

"Because of the disapproving expression on your face. Do you not care for the wine?"

"I don't know. I haven't tasted it yet."

"Why not? Are you afraid it might soften your mood? Make you look more kindly on the world in general, and me in particular?"

"I don't know what you're talking about. There's nothing wrong with my mood."

"Try again, *cara*," he said softly. "The perma-pout is impossible to miss and suits you no better than that outfit you're wearing." He stepped closer, and had the audacity to brace his calf against her, just below where the hem of her dress ended. "What exactly have I done, that has you looking as if you'd like to see me hanging by the neck from the nearest tree?"

The texture of his warm, hair-roughened skin against her bare knees stole her breath away. She wanted to let her legs fall apart until he was touching her inner thighs, and no sooner had such a shocking thought taken shape than her body responded with a ripple of longing. Oh, he was bad for her!

"The fact that you're taking unpardonable liberties, for a start!" she said weakly. "Remove your leg at once."

"I'm afraid I can't. It's attached to the rest of me."

"You know perfectly well what I mean, Matteo," she said, with a fraction more starch. "Stop behaving like a naughty child."

"Stop behaving like a Victorian governess." His gaze caressed her face, slid down her throat. "Did you think that, by dressing as you have, I would forget what lies underneath all that concealing fabric?'

"This might come as a shock, Matteo, but you actually had nothing to do with my choice of clothing. I had no idea you were going to be here today."

"Yet here I am, anyway, and you can't ignore the fact, no matter how much you try." He pressed a little closer until the length of his shin was aligned against hers. "Shall I tell you what I want to do with your virginal little dress?"

"No," she said, fighting to quell the hot flash of sensation he'd sent streaking through her body.

"I want to undo each of its prim little buttons until it falls open to reveal your beautiful breasts. I want to lift its skirt, bury my fingers in your warm, soft flesh, and stroke you until you whimper against my mouth and beg me to make love to you."

He was already making love to her! She was quivering all over with anticipation, and she was afraid to stand up because she was sure the rush of heat between her legs would leave its damp imprint on her skirt for everyone to see!

"Stop it!" she begged. "What if the others hear you?"

"They won't. Look at them. They've forgotten we're here."

He angled his body in such a way that she could see Corinna holding court. *Your grandfather's quite smitten,* Stephanie remembered her grandmother saying, and it was pretty clear he wasn't the only one. Her father was hanging on the widow's every word, and Victor was just about drooling. Even Drew had fallen under her spell.

"Just as well nobody's paying any mind to us," Stephanie said with a hard-won attempt at indifference. "I don't imagine your…*girlfriend* would care to know you're trying to seduce another woman on her turf."

Matteo stepped back, just enough to leave her knees so bereft of his warmth that a shiver stole over her. "I don't much like your choice of words," he stated coolly. "Corinna would be the first to admit she is long past the age where anyone could mistake her for a girl. But she *is* a lady, she *is* very much my friend, and I demand that you respect that. If you are jealous of her—and it would appear from your vitriolic tone that you are—it must be because she is such a generous and accomplished hostess who would never dream of belittling a guest in the way that you seem determined to belittle her."

Smarting, Stephanie said, "You're in no position to demand anything of me, Matteo. And just for the record, I am not jealous of *Signora* Russo. Frankly, I don't care how you define your relationship with her. Call her whatever you like. But a person would have to be blind not to see that she acts as if she owns you!"

"Perhaps she does," he said enigmatically. "The question is, why do you care?"

"Because I hoped you aspired to be something more than a rich woman's resident gigolo!"

The blood drained from his face and, aghast at what she'd said, at the venom and insult which had tripped so glibly from her lips, she clapped a hand to her mouth.

What in the world had possessed her?

She raised her eyes to meet his, mutely begging for forgiveness. But, unmoved by her consternation, he stepped even farther back and pierced her with a look so loaded with disgust that she withered inside.

She wanted to apologize, to tell him she'd spoken without thought and didn't mean a word she'd uttered. But as though sensing her intent, he forestalled her. *"Enough!"* he said with deadly, controlled emphasis. *"You have said enough!"*

The chill he left behind, as he stalked back to the rest

of the group, invaded Stephanie from head to toe. Feeling positively ill, she staggered to her feet and went in the opposite direction, toward the steps, desperate to escape before anyone noticed. She couldn't possibly face Matteo or Corinna with any sort of equanimity—not then, and perhaps not ever.

Shading her eyes, she stared down at the pool, at the dizzying panorama of lawn and flowers, of sea and sky. Where was Simon? She could not, *dare* not, leave without him.

A narrow, elegant hand closed over her arm. "Your little boy is safe, Stephanie," Corinna said. "He cannot wander far. Come sit with me, and let us get to know one another a little."

"I'd rather…I don't think…!" Dangerously close to tears, Stephanie stopped, pressed her fingers to her lips, and took a deep breath before trying again. "I don't think I can relax until I find him."

"Then we will go searching together."

"No, please!" She couldn't look at the other woman, couldn't bear the kindness and warmth she heard in her voice. "I wouldn't dream of taking you away from your other guests."

"But you are my guest, also, and are, it would appear, distressed. And that, in turn, distresses me."

"I'm just a little…on edge. The cliff is very steep, and Simon isn't used to—"

"Enough," Corinna said—the very same word Matteo had used, but spoken with such a wealth of compassion that Stephanie was filled with new shame. "First, we look for your son, then you and I will sit quietly and enjoy another glass of wine together, and leave the others to keep an eye on Simon until lunch is served. Come, *cara*. The butterfly garden is this way, and that's undoubtedly where we will find him."

She led the way down the steps and past Guido's cage. *"Ciao! E sposato?"* the parrot inquired coyly.

"We are neither of us married anymore," Corinna observed, directing Stephanie through a gap in the hedge next to the cage. "We are both alone, which gives us much in common, Stephanie. But unlike me, you have your son." Corinna lifted her shoulders in a regretful shrug. "Alas, my husband was not able to give me a child."

Mine, either! Stephanie thought, a pang of guilty fear slicing through her. If Corinna discovered that the boy she was helping to find was really Matteo's son, would she keep the secret, or would loyalty to Matteo compel her to share the news with him?

As though divining something of Stephanie's thoughts, Corinna said, "You met Matteo when he came to Canada, and yet you did not remain in contact with him. Did you not consider him your friend, Stephanie?"

"We knew each other for only a very short time— hardly long enough to form a friendship."

"Then you missed a rare opportunity. I cannot conceive of life without his friendship. He has been such a source of comfort and strength to me in the years since I lost my husband."

No doubt! Stephanie glanced across a swath of emerald lawn to where the car Matteo had driven the night before stood outside an open garage. "When did your husband die?"

"Eight years ago," Corinna said, following her gaze. "Do you see your son up there? If so, he misunderstood my directions."

"No, I was admiring the car," she said. "Is it yours?"

"Yes. If you would like to drive it while you are here—"

So he used her car! And what else? "No, thank you."

She shied away from the offer as if Corinna had suggested she swim with man-eating sharks. "I wouldn't be comfortable driving in such unfamiliar territory."

The widow laughed and led the way through another opening in the elaborately carved hedge. "I understand! Our traffic on Ischia is a little *matto*—crazy, as you'd say in English. Look, there is your son, exactly where I expected we'd find him."

They'd entered an enclosed garden alive with movement and birdsong. Butterflies hovered in the lavender-scented air, and flitted among a profusion of bright flowers. Simon crouched on the pedestal of a stone birdbath, half dozing in the sunshine.

"I should have made him wear a hat," Stephanie said, worriedly. "He's not used to such heat."

"You're lucky that he tans quickly and doesn't burn," Corinna remarked, as he ran over to join them. "He could pass for an Italian with such skin."

In many other ways, too, if truth be known! And Corinna, with her sharp eye, seemed the kind to notice details someone less observant might miss, which was reason enough for Stephanie to avoid her in the future. She'd worked too hard protecting her son's true paternity, to allow a passing stranger to uncover it.

"It's good that we found you," the widow teased, catching Simon by the hand. "Your poor mama was worried that you'd fallen into the sea. Are you hungry, *signor?*"

He nodded.

"Good. That is as it should be. Did you see lots of butterflies and birds?"

"Yes, but I didn't find the fishpond."

"Then you'll have to come back another day. There is much here that a young man your age would like to explore. Now let us hurry. How fast can you run, my beautiful boy?''

''Very fast,'' he said.

But Stephanie, following at a slower pace and watching, was terribly afraid there was no way either of them could outrun a past which suddenly seemed bent on catching up with them.

CHAPTER FIVE

AFTER the Leylands left, Baptiste brought a fresh pot of espresso out to the terrace. Once she'd served it and they were alone again, Corinna took her cup, stretched out in her favorite sun chaise, and said to Matteo, "You have a very unhappy face, *caro*. Care to tell me why?"

"You have very beautiful legs," he replied, not about to get into it with her, "and I'd much rather talk about them."

"My legs are exactly as they were two hours ago. You, however, are not. Before our guests arrived, you were relaxed and in good spirits. Yet by the time we sat down to lunch, you appeared troubled, and so angry that you barely touched the very excellent mussels I'd ordered, and which you normally enjoy immensely. Even now, you are brooding."

She was right. Out of sight didn't necessarily mean out of mind, and Stephanie's stinging remark had stayed with him. It infuriated him—not that she'd said what she had, but that he gave a damn. He should have known better than to think she might have changed. "I'd forgotten that I have a limited tolerance for the Leylands," he said. "Too much of their company turns my stomach."

"I found Anna and Brandon Leyland thoroughly charming."

"Oh, the grandparents are different. They're wonderful people and I'm very fond of them. Andrew's pretty decent, too."

"But you dislike his father and brother, the *Signors* Bruce and Victor?"

Matteo curled his lip in distaste. "I loathe them."

"Because?"

"Because they're bloated with self-importance, jump to unwarranted conclusions, and hold opinions on everything under the sun, regardless of whether or not they know the first thing of what they're talking about."

"They were agreeable enough to me, today."

"Don't be fooled by that, Corinna. They saw how you live, how you dress, how you entertain—all things which, in their eyes, made you socially acceptable." He grimaced. "And of course, it didn't hurt any that you're easy on the eye. But despite your looks, if *you'd* been the one serving the meal, instead of Baptiste, they wouldn't have spared you a second glance. If they'd seen you in the market buying fruit, or down on the quay choosing fish for dinner tonight, they'd have dismissed you as a nobody."

"I'm not so naive, Matteo!" she said, with a smile. "I know what it was that impressed them, but that merely makes them shallow and rather foolish in my eyes. Hardly worth the energy you expend on hating them, surely? And the mother, Vivienne, seemed a sweet and gentle soul."

"I'd respect her a whole lot more if she stood up to them once in a while. But she's a willing doormat. Her husband and eldest son treat her abominably, wipe their feet on her every chance they get, and she lets them get away with it every time."

"And the other one?"

"Other one?" He feigned confusion. "You mean the daughter, Stephanie?"

Corinna regarded him over the rim of her cup and said softly, "Let's not play games with one another, Matteo! We both know very well that I do."

"Oh, she's got attitude to spare and is never happier

than when she's shooting off her mouth! Comes by it naturally, of course. Takes after her father.''

''I disagree. I sensed in her much tension, a certain nervous edge, but not the arrogance you suggest. Nor did I detect any of this antipathy toward her that you show now. Rather, I felt the two of you were strongly attracted to one another and trying very hard to deny it.''

''You're imagining things. Mrs. Stephanie Leyland-Owen, or whatever she's calling herself these days, isn't my type.''

''It would be comforting to believe that, but I saw—''

''What you saw, Corinna,'' he cut in grimly, ''was a group of people related by blood, and two concerned, elderly relatives doing their utmost to unite them all into one big, happy family.''

''An admirable ambition, I'd say.''

''But one doomed to failure, because both Bruce and Victor's interest in family starts and ends with their ancestors' achievements.''

''*Ancestors?*'' Obviously puzzled, Corinna wrinkled her nose. ''I don't understand. What do dead people have to do with anything?''

''Apparently, in the 1800s, both Brandon and Anna's great-great-grandfathers rose to political acclaim in Canada, with close blood ties to equally prominent statesmen in the U.S. Why else do you think the lofty Professors Bruce and Victor Leyland specialize in nineteenth century North American history at their respective universities, if not because it affords them the chance to drop their family names into their lectures, at every turn?''

''How silly, and how pathetic! But Andrew and Stephanie are cut from different cloth, yes?''

''Andrew is,'' Matteo admitted. ''He's an independent thinker, an architect whose only interest in the past is the esthetic design of its buildings. But Stephanie...'' He lifted his shoulders in a shrug. "Stephanie might like to think she's her own person, but the reality is, she bends over backward to avoid displeasing her father. Hell, she even married a university professor she didn't really love, because he was enough like her father that he was bound to meet with approval."

"You speak as if you know her well."

"Yes. Better than I care to."

Corinna sipped her coffee and took pains to place the fragile cup and saucer on the glass table beside her chaise. Then, staring out across the Bay of Naples, she said with studied casualness, "You and I have never discussed this openly, Matteo, but I think you know that my affection for you runs deep."

"Ah, Corinna!" he began, uncomfortable at the turn in the conversation. "Don't—!"

"I won't," she assured him. "I have no wish to embarrass you or myself. I mention it only as a preface to this request: please describe to me, exactly, your relationship with Stephanie, and trust that my interest stems not from unseemly curiosity or resentment, but out of loyalty and true friendship toward you."

Corinna was the most discreet and sensitive person he knew, no more given to meddling in his past affairs than he was to broadcasting the details surrounding them. That she should suddenly pose such a personal question, and do it so frankly, compelled him to respond with equal candor. "We were lovers."

"I suspected as much." Her shoulders lifted in a faint sigh, and she lowered her eyes briefly, before raising them again to meet his. "How did her parents react to your associating with her?"

"They weren't aware of it. She made sure of that."

"But they must have known she was spending time with you."

"No. They lived in Toronto. I met her in Bramley Point, some two hundred miles northeast of the city, where her grandparents owned—still do own—lakeside property. She always spent part of each summer with them because she loved riding, and they kept very fine horses."

"So you were both there at the same time, living in the same house?"

"No. Even I had enough decency not to abuse my hosts' hospitality by deflowering their nineteen year-old granddaughter under their roof."

She let out a tiny gasp. "Are you saying, Stephanie was…?"

"A virgin? Yeah." He looked away, unable to meet the silent censure in Corinna's gaze. "I know! I should have been shot. But she was sweet and lovely, and desperate to be loved. Corinna, you have no idea how irresistible a combination that is to a man of twenty-five, who thinks he knows all the answers just because he has the sexual appetite of a young bull, and a pocketful of condoms handy whenever he needs them."

"I am not sitting in judgment, my friend. I know you didn't coerce Stephanie, that she came to you of her own free will. Go on with your story. How long were you together?"

"Five, maybe six weeks. I stayed in an apartment above the stables, she came there to ride her horse, we were alone…you can fill in the rest, I'm sure. Not a very pretty story, is it?"

"But you were in love with each other, yes?"

"Not I. Falling in love at twenty-five wasn't part of my grand life plan. But she said she was in love with me, and I was egotistical enough to believe her. Then, one day, her family showed up and stayed for nearly a week. And suddenly, Stephanie didn't know me anymore. When her father and brothers came with her to go riding one morning, I was already there, at the other end of the stables where Brandon kept his workshop, and she wouldn't so much as look in my direction."

"You think she was embarrassed?"

"I know damn well she was!"

"Because you were lovers?"

"No," he said harshly. "Because I was up to my eyebrows in grease and grime, and surrounded by bits and pieces of machinery. I didn't project the right aristocratic image."

"But she knew who you really were, what your family stood for in Italy."

"Uh-uh! She assumed I was a marble quarrier from Carrara, sent by my employer to investigate an unpatented invention designed to cut granite. And, loosely speaking, I was exactly that, if you consider my father and grandfather owned all shares in our company at that time, and I was still learning the business."

"And you saw no reason to enlighten her? To let her know you were heir to a fortune?"

"Good God, no! You remember how I was, back then, Corinna: proud, stubborn, and hell-bent on making my own way without relying on my family's name or wealth to get me where I wanted to go. It was the main reason I volunteered to spend the summer in Canada, a new world where all men are equal and the tedium of being rich and powerful carried less clout—or so I thought, until I met Bruce Leyland."

Yes," she said with a quiet laugh. "I remember very well. You were also headstrong, charming, and handsome, and had such a way with the ladies that mothers used to lock up their unmarried daughters when you came to Ischia for the summer. It would seem that *Signor* Brandon should have done the same with Stephanie."

"Maybe he should." He squinted into the bright afternoon sun because it was less painful than looking back at his murky past. "I showed up at his place, determined to prove I amounted to more than an aristocratic name, that I was a man in my own right. Instead, I showed myself to be ultimately as callous and cruel as my medieval ancestors in the way that I cast Stephanie aside when I'd had my way with her. I was a fool to think I could shed my heritage like a snake shedding its skin."

"Don't be so hard on yourself. Young men make mistakes—it's the nature of the beast. Continue with your story instead. What happened with Bruce Leyland, that you're still so full of bitterness?"

"On the Saturday, Anna invited me to join them for a family barbecue. My first instinct was to refuse, but then I thought, *Why the hell not? I'm every bit as good as they are!*

"So I showed up, all shaved and polished until I shone. But I might just as well have been sporting a two-day growth of beard, and been covered in dirt, for all the good it did me. Bruce Leyland treated me as if I was some Third World refugee looking for a hand-out. As for Victor, I half expected him to toss his food scraps at me."

"And you still didn't set them in their place by revealing your true identity?"

"Are you kidding? I didn't owe either of them any explanations. In any case, I was having too much fun playing the dumb, swarthy foreigner who didn't know which fork to use. When Brandon mentioned that I thought his invention had the potential for a computerized application which could revolutionize the marble cutting industry, the good Professors Leyland laughed in my face and sneeringly told me that I was out of my league; that it took education and brains to understand how computers worked."

"*Per carita,* but for supposedly intelligent men, they

were fools to underestimate you! Do you suppose they now acknowledge that you were light-years ahead of the times in your thinking?"

"I neither know nor care. What *does* intrigue me is that you do—care, that is, about something that no longer matters. Why, Corinna?"

She swung her legs to the ground and drifted to the edge of the terrace. "Because, whether or not you're prepared to admit it, you still care about your Stephanie, *caro*," she said, standing with her back to him and staring out across the sea. "You care so deeply that I worry for you."

"Don't lose sleep on my account. Stephanie and I are a thing of the past."

She shook her head. "I suspect not. Did you continue the affair after her family left?"

"No."

"She never came to your apartment again?"

"Sure she did," he said, unable to contain the bitterness in his voice. "The minute her parents hit the road, she was ready to hit the sheets again. Or, more accurately, ready for another roll in the hay."

"And...?"

"And it didn't happen. I told her it was over."

"And she accepted it, just like that?"

"Not just like that. She cried, and begged me to change my mind. Said she was sorry she'd acted the way she had, but that it was to shield me because she'd been afraid of how her father might react if he'd found out about us. *Shield me*, Corinna—as if I was some coward willing to hide behind a woman's skirts! What kind of a man did she take me for?"

"Don't you see, she wasn't belittling your courage! A woman in love will do whatever she feels she has to do, to protect her man."

"I didn't want or need her protection."

"No, you wanted and needed her, but your pride wouldn't let you have her. Which of you, I wonder, has paid the higher price for that?"

"Not I," he said. "Stephanie made her choices, and I made mine. And once I've made up my mind on something, there's no changing it. You know that, Corinna."

"Yes, I do. But I also know a man driven by uncertainty and regret, when I see one." Corinna spun back to face him. "And right now, I'm looking at him. Go to her, *caro*," she begged, coming toward him and grasping his hands. "Talk to her. Sort things out."

"Not a chance," he said flatly, refusing even to consider the idea. "We're over! Done!"

"This reminds me of when you were still a girl, and used to spend the summers with us." Anna Leyland patted the cushion beside her on the silk-upholstered sofa, inviting Stephanie to sit. "Afternoon tea and cake in the drawing room was a daily ritual I very much enjoyed, back then. It's not quite the same here, of course."

"Not quite." Forcing herself to sound a lot more cheerful than she felt, Stephanie joined her grandmother. "No Upper Canada antiques, British India rugs, or old family photos scattered around. None of those wonderful little scones Esther used to bake, either."

"But very fine furnishings and paintings, nevertheless, and lovely cool marble floors underfoot. The tiramisu's nothing to sneeze at, either."

Stephanie kicked off her sandals and tucked her feet under her. "I think Sunday brunch was my favorite time," she said dreamily. "Mimosas on the veranda, eggs Benedict and *café au lait,* and Vivaldi drifting out from the stereo in the parlor."

"Memories are wonderful things, aren't they?" her

grandmother replied gently. "They keep us connected to our past."

Which wasn't necessarily a good thing! Stephanie thought, flooded again with other recollections—of innocence, and a time before her life was burdened by guilt and shame and lies. She had been young, carefree, and desperately in love with an unsuitable man. If her father had known she'd lost her virginity to her grandparents' stone mason, he'd have killed him and her both. "I suppose they can be, yes."

Her grandmother fanned herself with a folded linen napkin and eyed Stephanie lovingly. "But they aren't always enough, are they, darling child?"

"Enough?" Echoes of Matteo using the same word rang discordantly through her mind, and she shrank all over again at the absolute contempt with which he'd uttered it. "Enough for what?"

"To make you happy."

"I'm happy." To prove it, she produced a smile which left her face feeling as if it were being stretched apart by invisible wires. "Why wouldn't I be?"

"I was hoping you'd tell me before your mother joins us. I'm fully aware that you don't feel able to speak freely in front of her." Anna lifted the elegant silver teapot and poured Earl Grey into translucent porcelain cups.

"Well, I don't care for the way my father treats her, if that's what you mean. And I have absolutely no patience with Victor's pretentious posturing. But I'm trying not to let it interfere with the reason we're here. I know how much you want this family reunion to work, Grandmother."

"That's true, but I realized long ago that the only person who can change the way your father treats your mother is Vivienne herself. Until she does, I'm afraid there's nothing you or I can do but accept the situation.

As for Victor, he's like a gnat. Irritating, but important only if you allow him to be.'' Anna added a sliver of lemon to the tea and passed a cup and saucer to Stephanie. ''How was your date, last night?'

Taken aback at the sudden change of subject, Stephanie said cautiously, ''Very nice, thank you.''

''You and Matteo got along well, did you?''

''Famously.'' Most of the time. Except for when she'd lied to him.

''Then what went wrong between him and you today?''

She turned away from her grandmother's probing gaze, hoping to hide the blush warming her cheeks. ''What makes you think anything did?''

''I was watching the interaction between the two of you. I saw how the temperature went from scorching to freezing in the blink of an eye. And I know full well the reason you're wishing you'd never come to Ischia has nothing to do with your father or brother, and everything to do with Matteo De Luca, so don't try to convince me otherwise. What was it, Stephanie? Did Matteo insult you in some fashion?''

The silence spun out, as her grandmother waited patiently for her to reply. ''No,'' Stephanie finally admitted, her voice low and ashamed. ''I insulted him.''

''Did he deserve it?''

''No. What I said, what I…accused him of, was indefensible.''

''So what are you going to do to put things right between you?''

''Nothing,'' she said.

''No apology? No explanation for behaving as you did?''

''Matteo made it pretty plain that he wasn't interested, either in an apology, or an explanation—even if I could come up with one that made any sense.''

"That may well be the case, and perhaps you don't deserve to be excused for whatever it was you said. But *something* provoked you enough to speak out of character, Stephanie, and asking for his understanding might at least enable you to forgive yourself. We've all said things we shouldn't, at times. What counts is being big enough to admit it."

She heaved a long sigh. "There's so much more to this than you realize, Grandmother. It's…complicated."

"Because he was your first love? What's complicated about that?"

"You *knew?*"

"Well, I'd have had to be blind and decidedly stupid *not* to, darling!"

Stephanie's jaw dropped and she went cold all over. She'd been so careful, waiting until her grandparents' bedroom was in darkness before sneaking out of the house to meet Matteo, and always made sure she was back in her own bed long before dawn. "And you didn't try to stop me?"

Her grandmother laughed. "How do you stop a nineteen-year-old girl from turning pink around the edges, every time a certain handsome young man's name is mentioned, or he puts in an appearance?"

"Oh…*that!*" Another blush chased away the chill.

"Yes, that. What did you think I meant?"

The blush turned to fire and spread up her neck to envelop her face in flames. "I…don't know. I just feel like such a fool."

"Because you once fell in love with Matteo De Luca, or because you're afraid you might do so again?"

She closed her eyes, knowing Anna was right. Seeing Matteo again had revived all those old, wild feelings, and after years of order and relative tranquility, her life was suddenly spinning out of control again. She remembered how much she'd loved him, and telling herself all that was in the past didn't amount to a hill of beans beside the jealousy she'd known when she'd seen how close he and Corinna were.

It wasn't a question of her falling in love with him again; it was whether she'd ever stopped loving him to begin with.

"Oh, Grandmother!" she sighed. "Is it *so* obvious?"

"I'm afraid it is. Which brings me again to the question of what you plan to do about it."

"There's nothing I can do. It's clear he doesn't feel the same way about me."

"Perhaps because you're so busy throwing up barriers that he hasn't had a chance to get to know the real you."

"It's just as well. He'd find the real me even more detestable than the one he thinks he knows."

"Stephanie, for a mature and intelligent woman, you sometimes come out with the most absurd statements! The man has pursued you from the minute you set foot on this island. He's shown himself willing to take a chance. Why can't you meet him halfway?"

Because I'm afraid! "Because it's too late. I made sure of that this afternoon."

"As long as you have life and breath, it's never too late." Anna took Stephanie's face between her hands. "You say you don't want to disappoint me, that you want this to be a happy, memorable time for your grandfather and me, something that will give him the peace of mind he longs for so desperately. Well, darling child, paying lip service to the idea isn't enough. You've got to do your part in *making* it happen."

"By throwing myself at Matteo when he's made it clear he wants nothing more to do with me? That's blackmail, Grandmother!"

"I prefer to call it sound advice." Glancing at the gilt carriage clock on the table at her side, she rose from the couch. "Go to him, darling," she urged. "Talk to him. Sort things out. What do you have to lose?"

CHAPTER SIX

WHAT did she have to lose?

Just about everything, that's what! the cautious, practical side of Stephanie's personality warned. *It isn't only about you and Matteo, and falling in love, anymore; it's about Simon. If you rekindle that early passion and find it to be more durable this time around, you're going to have to choose truth over deceit, or live in fear of discovery for the rest of your life. And truth, my dear, isn't all it's cracked up to be. It could spell disaster and heartbreak for everyone concerned. You're better off sticking with the lies.*

Yet how much protection did they really offer? she wondered. Drew had taken Simon beachcombing earlier. What if they happened to meet Matteo and, in the course of idle conversation, one or the other let slip something to arouse his suspicion?

Already, he'd remarked on how big Simon was for his age. What if the thought occurred again, and he came right out and asked when Simon was born? What if, even as she paced the villa's upper balcony envisioning the worst, it was actually happening, and her son was spilling information which would inadvertently reveal her closely-guarded secret?

She shivered in the late afternoon heat, and scanned the empty garden. Earlier, she'd felt the blistering sting of Matteo's anger. How much deadlier it would be, should he ever learn that casting aspersions on his moral integrity was the least of her sins toward him!

Still, Anna's advice lingered, ripe with tempting possibilities. Might it not be worth giving him time to cool down, then going to him and apologizing? If he rebuffed her, she'd at least have the satisfaction of knowing she'd done the right thing, and have lost nothing but her pride. But if he welcomed a reconciliation, they both might have much, if not everything, to gain.

Could she do it? *Should* she?

Sighing, she raked another worried glance over the still-deserted garden. In the end, it all came back to Simon, a boy who'd unknowingly adopted his biological father as his new hero. She could make that father a permanent part of his life, if only she dared.

The trouble was, she had no control over the outcome of such a revelation. It might result in happy-ever-after, and it might not. Did she have the right to gamble on the reality of what she and her son already had, however imperfect that might be, for the sake of a highly improbable fairy-tale ending with the man whose paternal link to Simon had been the result of sheer bad luck? What if all she did was make matters worse?

Let sleeping dogs lie, some wise person once said, and perhaps she was better off clinging to that. Simon was not, after all, an unhappy boy; he wasn't insecure. There were male influences in his life, and there could be more, if her grandmother's hope for closer family ties actually materialized. True, he wished he had a father, but realistically, would he be any better off with one who lived half a world away?

Voices below jarred her out of her introspection and had her peering expectantly over the veranda railing. Relieved, she saw Drew chasing Simon as he raced through the garden, dodging behind the trees, leaping over flower beds, and doing his utmost to elude his uncle. He was laughing, happy, carefree—all the things a mother wanted to see in her child.

Forget Matteo, that wise, pragmatic inner voice counseled. *What you see right now, what you already have—this* is what your life's really all about.

But, ironically, no one else in the family was inclined to dismiss him so easily.

"Too blasted hot for golf," Bruce declared toward the end of dinner that evening, when asked how he and Victor had enjoyed their afternoon. "Decent of Corinna, though, to arrange for us to play at her club. We'll have to reciprocate in some way. Invite her over here for cocktails, or take her out somewhere for a meal. What did you all think of her, by the way?"

"Perfectly charming," Stephanie's grandfather said promptly. "Knows how to entertain. Obviously a woman of class and taste."

"But what the devil was De Luca doing there?" Victor drawled, his habitually supercilious tone more pronounced than usual.

"What he does best, I suspect. Latching onto someone with money." Bruce eased one finger under the collar of his dress shirt, and nodded for Gaetan, the *maggiordomo,* to refill his wine glass. "And from the look of him, he's persuading Corinna to part with plenty of hers. Did you see the watch he was wearing?"

"No," Victor snorted. "I kept any sort of contact with him, visual or otherwise, to a minimum. He's a damn sight too familiar with people beyond his station, if you ask me, kissing my grandmother and mother's hands, and draping himself all over Corinna."

"I rather liked having my hand kissed," Anna said mildly.

At that, a timid voice spoke up from the other end of the table. "So did I."

A stunned silence descended, and all eyes turned on

Vivienne. "Well, I did," she said, staring back defiantly. "It was quite…lovely. Very continental."

"Trust you to be taken in by a smooth operator!" her husband sneered.

"Well, Bruce, at least he showed some manners, which is more than can be said of you or Victor! I thought you both were very rude to him. I was embarrassed."

Victor's mouth dropped open and Stephanie's father looked thunderstruck. Recovering himself with some difficulty, he inquired coldly, "Are you drunk, Vivienne?"

"No." She twisted her opal dinner ring nervously. "I'm speaking my mind, for once."

"About time, too," Anna said approvingly. "And you're quite right, Vivienne. My son and grandson behaved disgracefully. Thank heavens Andrew and Stephanie were there to balance the scales."

But she hadn't done that, Stephanie thought miserably. She'd merely added insult to injury, and she owed it to herself, let alone Matteo, at least to put that much right.

She waited until Simon was tucked in for the night before following through on her resolve. By then, her grandparents had coaxed her mother and Drew into a round of bridge, and her father was engaged in a game of chess with Victor.

"I'm going out for a while," she told them, pausing in the entrance to the day salon.

Annoyed by the interruption, her father looked pointedly at the ormolu long-case clock in the corner and gave a disapproving sniff. "At this hour? It's almost ten o'clock."

"I'm not asking your permission, Father," she informed him tartly. "In fact, I wouldn't have bothered mentioning it at all, if it weren't that I need someone to keep an ear out for Simon. Grandmother, would you mind—?''

"I'll listen for him," her mother offered. "I'd love to baby-sit. It's something I've never been able to do before, with you both living so far away. Go out and have fun, Stephanie.''

Catching her grandmother's conspiratorial glance, Stephanie said, "Well, I'm hardly expecting that from…a stroll in the garden, but thanks anyway, Mother. I won't be gone long.''

"Take all the time you need," Anna said, her attempt to appear artless betrayed by the wicked twinkle in her eye. "We'll hold down the fort here.''

The trouble, Stephanie decided, descending the steps from the terrace to the garden, was that her grandmother had been born blessed with more than her fair share of optimism. It was the reason she'd coerced her dysfunctional family into this vacation-cum-reunion, and it was the reason she believed a sincere apology was all it took to repair a relationship, regardless of how badly damaged it might be.

Stephanie, though, doubted Matteo would respond quite so generously and her courage, which had been in short enough supply to begin with, lessened with every step that took her closer to his cottage. Still, her conscience wouldn't allow her to turn back. It was already burdened with enough guilt.

Except for the faraway murmur of the sea, the night air was still, and fragrant with flowers, but the moon had not yet risen above Mount Epomeo. The bulk of the mountain left the pergola swathed in darkness and, as she passed underneath, her foot became tangled in some sort of creeping vine which almost sent her sprawling.

Ahead, the dense shrubbery cast even thicker black pools of shadow across the path, and she wished she'd thought to carry a flashlight. She'd also have been better off to change into something more practical than the high-heeled sandals and ankle-length dress she'd worn at dinner. But Matteo's unflattering comments on her outfit at lunch had stung and, truth to tell for once, she wanted to leave behind a more favorable impression this time, since it might well turn out to be the *last* time they saw each other.

When she finally arrived at his cottage, her heart was hammering, her palms were damp, and what had seemed like the honorable thing to do, when she'd thought about it earlier, suddenly struck her as foolhardy and pointless— a sop to ease her troubled mind. As if apologizing for a verbal insult in any way compensated for the vastly greater sin of concealing Simon's paternity! If she were one-tenth as decent as she proclaimed herself to be, she'd tell Matteo everything he had a right to know, and let the chips fall where they may.

The upper floor of the house lay in darkness. However, his front door and the windows to either side of it stood open to the warm night, and flung golden prisms of lamplight into the water spilling from the courtyard fountain. At that, the faint hope that he might not be home died and, gritting her teeth, Stephanie approached the little gate set in the low wall surrounding the place. It opened with the merest click but, to her heightened awareness, the sound carried the weight of a thunderclap, and she froze with her hand on the latch, waiting for him to appear and demand an explanation for her showing up uninvited.

Instead, the night remained silent, leaving her wondering if perhaps he was already in bed. But surely, if that were the case, he'd have turned out the downstairs lights…unless he wasn't alone, and was so engrossed in entertaining a guest that he wouldn't have noticed if Mount Epomeo's dead volcanic peak had suddenly erupted.

The prospect filled Stephanie with such a wave of dismay that she tiptoed across the courtyard and, holding her breath, peeped through the uncurtained window to the right of the front door. Relief washed over her at what she discovered. The room beyond was deserted.

Of course, she had no business spying. Should either have announced herself or left, as anyone with a speck of self-respect would have. But somehow, even in absentia, Matteo brought out the worst in her. And so she lingered, at the mercy of insatiable curiosity.

A handsome rug, Savonnerie from the looks of it, covered most of the floor. Framed antique maps hung on the walls. A leather sofa flanked a small marble fireplace filled with an arrangement of dried flowers. Against the far wall, a desk held a lamp, and three decanters on a silver tray. On a coffee table, half-burned candles in marble holders shared space with an empty brandy snifter and a book. All very cozy, and so harmlessly reassuring that she stole past the front door to the other window.

It, though, had louvered shutters angled so that no one from the outside could see in—and heaven knew, she tried hard enough, pressing her face to the glass and squinting upward like the relentless voyeur she'd suddenly become.

Horrified at what her obsession with Matteo had reduced her to, she straightened and edged toward the front door, determined to put an end to all the nonsense. "Fish or cut bait, you idiot!" she scolded, reaching for the wrought iron bell chain hanging on the wall.

But before she could pull it, she found herself pinned from behind in the beam of a powerful flashlight. A second later, Matteo's disembodied voice floated through the garden. "If you're thinking of stealing the silver, *Signora,* you ought to know that the *polizia* on this island take a very dim view of pilfering tourists, especially women. I've heard that, as a warning to other like-minded foreigners, such thieves are imprisoned in chairs in a certain room in the *Castello Aragonese,* and left there to die.''

She should have been embarrassed, shocked, even frightened. And perhaps she was. Perhaps it was the volatile combination of all three that caused her to respond by wheeling around and, in a burst of fury as irrational as it was inappropriate, yell, "What the hell do you think you're doing, Matteo? Turn off that light!''

"Don't shout at me,'' he replied, unmoved, and aimed the lamp directly at her face. "And in case you haven't noticed, I'm not the one owing anybody explanations.''

Throwing up her hand to shield her eyes from the glare, she said heatedly, "I wasn't planning to steal anything, you fool! What kind of person do you think I am?''

"I wish I knew,'' he said, playing the beam slowly down her body. "Why don't you enlighten me, Stephanie?''

His voice was hoarse with suppressed emotion—anger, regret, sorrow? She couldn't tell. He was doing too good a job of masking his true feelings from her. Feeling utterly naked, utterly defenseless, and knowing she had no one to blame but herself, she said, "I will. Please, just turn that thing off, first.''

She heard a click, and promptly found herself blinded by darkness. "I'm waiting,'' he said.

"Well...um....''

"Yes?''

She drew in a frustrated breath. "It's not easy talking to someone I can't see, you know!''

The flashlight clicked on again, this time to reveal him lounging in a hammock slung between two sturdy flowering trees, and from where she stood, he looked to be half-naked. "Here I am in the flesh,'' he said, unaware of the irony of his reply, "and you've now run out of excuses. So, once again, I ask: why are you here?"

She dragged her gaze away from all that tantalizing male skin. "I wanted to apologize."

"For what? Snooping?"

"I wasn't snooping. I thought you might be... entertaining, and I didn't want to intrude."

"The only entertaining thing in these parts is you, Stephanie," he said, rolling out of the hammock to land lithely on his feet. "Try again."

He wasn't quite as naked as she'd first thought. He was simply shirtless. But his shorts, the same pair he'd worn at lunch, were unbuttoned at the waist, leaving them hanging so indecently low on his hips that it was a miracle they stayed up at all. The very idea that they might not, made her tingle in unmentionable places.

"I wasn't sure you were even home," she said raggedly, averting her eyes.

"So how did you plan to find out? By standing under the balcony and caroling, *Matteo, Matteo, wherefore art thou, Matteo?*"

She didn't need to look at him to know he found her highly amusing. "Don't you dare laugh at me!" she fumed. "Not after all the grief you've caused me!"

"I can't help myself, *cara.* You just don't seem able to open your mouth without putting both feet in it. As for causing grief, if anyone here's the injured party, I am." He came toward her, shaking his head dolefully and suddenly sounding anything but amused. "A gigolo shouldn't be capable of feelings, though, should he? His only interest lies in taking advantage of—"

"Matteo, please!" She felt thoroughly sick with shame and humiliation. "I don't know what came over me, this afternoon. My only excuse is that, sometimes, under pressure, people say things they don't really mean."

"True enough," he replied. "This afternoon, I told you I wanted to make love with you. Now I freely admit, that's no longer the case."

As if she wasn't already chagrined enough, he had to add that! "I hardly expected it would be."

"Of course you did, Stephanie," he drawled, stepping close enough to run an insolent finger down the side of her neck and along her shoulder to the braided silk straps holding up her dress. "That's why you showed up here in the first place, all dressed to kill. You wanted to see if you could knock off the competition."

"I don't know what you're talking about!"

"And that's the lamest and oldest lie of them all, *cara*. We both know *exactly* what—or, more accurately, *who*— I'm talking about. You're jealous of Corinna."

For a moment, she glared at him, full of self-righteous indignation. And then the fight went out of her. "Yes, I am," she admitted on a sigh, too weary to continue the charade. "I wish to heaven I weren't—that I didn't give a hoot who you're sleeping with."

"Well, now we're getting somewhere!" His voice softened, rolled over her like brandied honey. "Was it so very hard to confess your true feelings, for a change?"

"Yes. I don't want to care about you, Matteo. I don't want to go through all that misery again, when I leave here—wondering if you're kissing someone else, if you're touching her the way you once touched me, and whispering in *her* ear the words I thought you only ever intended for mine."

He moved closer still. Framed her face with his hands. His mouth was achingly close, his gaze in the dim light disturbingly intent. "Then live for the moment, and let tomorrow take care of itself."

"I can't."

"Why not?"

"Because I'm not like you. I can't just wipe my memory clean."

"And you think I can?" He smoothed his forefinger over her lips, pried them gently apart, and briefly inserted the tip into her mouth. "Think again, Stephanie," he purred.

A bolt of heat streaked through her and left her weak and trembling. He couldn't have invoked a more thrillingly erotic reaction if he'd kissed her deeply, or invaded her most secret and intimate flesh. "You did before," she said, her voice barely above a whisper.

"How do you know?"

"You left without saying goodbye. You never called, never wrote."

"It was for the best. I wasn't what you needed then."

"You're not what I need now."

He let go of her and stepped back a pace. "Then don't let me keep you. You've said what you came to say. Now go home."

How dearly she wished she could! But the message her brain tried transmitting to her legs went astray, and instead of turning and beating a fast retreat, she remained rooted to the spot.

"Not until you tell me one thing. Are you and Corinna lovers?"

"That's hardly any of your business, is it?"

"*Are* you?"

Ever so deliberately, he reached inside his khaki shorts to rearrange his underwear—and heaven only knew what else—then hauled them up around his waist and slowly fastened the button. "I might not be a gentleman by your standards, Stephanie," he drawled mockingly, fully aware that she watched his every move, dry-mouthed with fascination, "but I'm chivalrous enough not to kiss and tell."

"You're not a gentleman by anyone's standards!" she gasped, wrenching her gaze away.

"And that's why you were so attracted to me in the first place, isn't it? You got some sort of sadistic thrill from doing it with a peasant."

Doing it? She could have wept. He'd been her first and, in many ways, her only lover. She had given him more than her body; she'd trusted him with her heart and soul. Yet he dismissed what they'd been to one another as merely *doing it!* "No more than you did from *doing it* with a lady!" she spat.

"Really?" He circled her thoughtfully, his bare feet soundless on the paving stones, his skin gleaming coppery gold in the faint light. "Is that why you're really here—to put the theory to the test? See if we can still connect on the old level?"

"No!"

"Then I guess we've said everything there is to say." He held open the gate. *"Buona notte."*

Again, she tried to move her feet, and again they refused her. Her throat was thick was misery, her eyes burning with unshed tears. She was afraid to blink, for fear that they'd roll down her face and he'd see them.

Emotions raw and dangerously close to the surface, she sank down on the stone edge of the fountain. She'd coped with family estrangement, divorce, death; successfully juggled single parenthood and a career. But Matteo showed up out of the blue, and she fell apart at the seams.

He'd come back into her life less than a week ago. They'd spent only a few hours together. There were insurmountable obstacles lying between them. Yet she was on the brink of loving him again, and fighting her feelings left her so emotionally disjointed and fragile that she barely recognized herself.

Why did it have to be him living next door? she asked

herself bitterly. Why not some tall, dark, handsome stranger, instead of a man so familiar to her dreams that her heart could have identified him in a crowd of thousands?

Oblivious to her distress, he pushed away from the gate. "Take your time," he said, strolling past her toward the house.

Almost immediately, the front door closed, the downstairs grew dark, and a light shone from an upstairs window. And still she sat there, knowing that what she *wanted* to do, and what she *ought* to do, weren't one and the same, and fighting to make the right, the wiser choice.

At length, the battle over even though the war was far from won, she stood up and started the long, difficult journey home. Not to the villa next door, but to where her heart belonged.

He hadn't locked the door. Nor had he gone to bed. He leaned against the wall at the top of the staircase, waiting.

"I was beginning to think you'd never make up your mind," he said, holding out his hand. "*Avanti*—come, *innamorata!* We've fought the inevitable long enough."

CHAPTER SEVEN

JUDGING by the way she clung to the banister and took each stair one at a time, dragging her feet as if some invisible anchor weighed her down, Matteo half expected she'd change her mind.

"Avanti," he said again, this time gentling his tone to make the word less a command than a soothing invitation.

Slowly she drew closer, until at last her fingertips brushed his. Grasping them, he pulled her the rest of the way and into his arms. She collapsed against him, as spent and shaken as if she'd climbed Mount Epomeo in her flimsy high heels.

"Was that so very difficult?" he asked her.

She lifted her head to meet his gaze, and to his dismay he saw panic in her eyes. "Yes," she said tremulously. "It was one of the hardest things I've ever had to do."

"You do not trust me?"

"I don't trust myself."

He stroked her hair, loving the cool, silken feel of it slipping between his fingers. "Why not?"

"Because I forget to be careful with you. You make me say things better kept to myself. You make me want things I can't have."

"How do you know you can't have them? Have you asked?"

She pressed her lips together and didn't answer.

"Have you?"

"No."

"Why not?"

"Because I already know the answer."

"Which is?"

She hesitated just long enough for him to know she was about to lie—or, at the very least, tell only a partial truth. "That *you* don't really want me. You told me so, not half an hour ago."

"And if I've changed my mind? If I spoke in haste, out of anger and hurt pride?"

"You could change your mind again," she said, her voice tight with anguish. "I could make you angry again."

"What do I have to do to reassure you, Stephanie?"

"Convince me you care enough that nothing I've said or done in the past will change how you feel about me now."

Unconditional acceptance? He wasn't prepared to go that far quite yet. But, "I have always cared, Stephanie," he said gravely. "Enough to leave you before. Enough to ask you to stay with me tonight, in the sincere belief that we have a shot at a new beginning."

She shifted restlessly in his arms, a beautiful butterfly tempted by danger to ignore the safety of flight. Though unintentionally arousing, the whisper of silk against his skin, the movement of her breasts sliding against his chest, stirred his body to hunger. "You know that I can't," she sighed. "I have to think of Simon—"

He brought his mouth to her ear, nibbled lightly on the diamond stud in her lobe. "For a few hours only," he coaxed. "You'll be home before sunrise. Simon will never know. No one will."

"I shouldn't," she faltered.

But she did. She let him kiss the side of her neck, and her shoulder, and her throat. She trembled all over when he pushed down the straps of her dress. She whimpered his name when he dipped his tongue in the sweet, warm valley between her breasts. And when he dropped to his knees, taking her dress with him and leaving it puddled around her feet, then settled his mouth at her bare, narrow waist, she let out a gasp and pressed her hands to the back of his head, holding him captive against her.

He inhaled the delicate, unforgettable scent of her. Ran his palms up the back of her thighs. Hooked his thumbs inside the front of her underpants. Parted the soft, full curves between her legs, and touched her.

She stiffened. Knotted her hands in his hair. Let out a stifled gasp.

He trailed his mouth down her flat, quivering belly and brought it to rest against the triangle of fabric covering her womanhood. Blew a long, damp breath against her. With his tongue drew a wet, lazy circle on the satin, then took it between his teeth and tugged it down her legs, one excruciating centimeter after another. By the time it reached her ankles, she was begging for him, her voice drowning in tears, and the aroused, honeyed taste of her was driving him mad.

Lunging to his feet, he caught her up in his arms and strode the short length of the hall to his room. Her dress remained on the floor at the top of the stairs. Somewhere in transit, her satin underpants slipped off. When he finally laid her on the bed, she wore only her bra and one shoe. He made very short work of both.

"There's something you have to know," she muttered, rising up one elbow. "I shouldn't have waited until now to tell you, but I can't let it go on—"

He stepped out of his shorts and briefs. Pulled open the drawer in the nightstand. "Don't worry, *cara*. You won't get pregnant."

Sinking down on the mattress, she pressed a hand to her mouth, and stared at him, dazed and…something else…something along the lines of *fearful*. As if she thought he might harm her in some way. "Matteo," she begged unevenly, "please listen! This is important."

He flattened his hand beneath her left breast, directly over her heart. It fluttered as wildly as a trapped bird. "The only thing important at this moment is whether or not you want me to make love to you. If I've misread the signals, tell me now, Stephanie, because I'm not made of marble. Much more of this…." He kissed her inner elbow, the hollow of her throat, the corner of her mouth. "Much more of this," he finished, dragging the warning past the hunger ravaging him, "and I won't be able to stop."

"I want you," she wailed softly, covering his hand. "You know I do. But you might not want me if—"

"I'm very clear about what I want," he said, bending over her as she lay on the bed, her beautiful body dappled in lamplight. "I have been from the second you I saw you in the garden, last week."

"It's not quite that simple," she protested, even as her hands strayed up to caress his shoulders. "There's so much you don't know."

"It's exactly that simple. This…" He brushed his mouth over her nipples and past her navel to the top of her thighs. "…is about you and me, and no one else. Stop trying to turn us into something complicated."

"But we *are* complicated!"

"Shut up, *tesoro*," he murmured hoarsely, bringing his mouth back to hover over hers, and slipping his hand between her legs. However morally bound she felt to resist him, she was deliciously sleek and ready for him. "Let me love you, instead. Then we'll talk until dawn, if you wish."

"Oh!" she moaned anxiously, clamping her thighs together and snaring his hand hard against her, as the first faint tremors of orgasm echoed through her body. *"Oh!"*

He moved his finger, found the firm bud of flesh nestled at her core, and circled it expertly, remembering as if it were just yesterday that they'd last made love, how to bring her to release. Her body arched, a slim, flexible bow of sweet golden skin stretched taut over finely-fashioned bone and muscle. She cried out, and clung to him, her body convulsing in a series of spasms that shook the bed.

"Now!" she pleaded, her hands racing down his torso to cradle him. "Oh, *please,* Matteo, come to me now!"

"Sì, la mia innamorata," he ground out, suddenly teetering on the edge of control, and grabbed the condom from the nightstand. She reached out to help him—a loving, generous act, at once exquisitely cruel and magnificently exciting.

And then he was where he'd wanted to be, from the moment she'd walked back into his life. Buried inside her. Sheathed tightly in the hot, sleek confines of her body.

Desire ran free, exploding within him so fiercely that he almost came before he'd had time to savor the moment. Shuddering, he partially withdrew, willing his flesh to subjugation. At twenty-five, premature ejaculation might have been excusable, but it was not the way a man of thirty-five pleased a woman.

Because she was urging him on with feather-light touches to his groin, he took her hands and pinned them on the pillow above her head. *"Tu rallentari!"* he groaned. "Slow down, my Stephanie!"

At once, she locked her legs around his waist and, as he delved deep within her a second time, brought her hips up to meet his thrust. More than his control slipped, then; the entire world fell away. Swearing, sweating, fighting a battle he hadn't a prayer of winning, he cushioned her small firm buttocks with his palms, welding her to him as they tumbled together down an abyss so deep and dark and thrilling that he didn't care if they never hit bottom.

Then, it was over, and in the span of that too-short, lavishly exquisite agony, the man he'd been, lived—and he died. With the last of his seed spilling free from his body, so, too, did all the constants by which, until that moment, he'd steered his destiny. Stripped of power and direction and purpose, unsure of what lay ahead, he collapsed on top of her.

At length, with a mighty effort, he raised his head to look at her. Her eyes had turned violet with passion, and a delicate flush stained her throat and face. "You haven't changed," he told her huskily. "Say what you will, but in all the ways that count, you're still the same girl who gave herself to me that long-ago summer. Still full of passion and fire. Still so desirable that I look back now and wonder what kind of fool I had to be, to leave you as I did."

She turned her head aside and wiped a hand over the dew of perspiration filming her upper lip. "My body's not the same," she panted. "Childbirth has taken its toll."

Rolling to lie beside her, he tracked his finger over a tiny silvery mark near her navel, a souvenir of her pregnancy, but one so faint as to be barely discernible. "It has made you more beautiful."

She managed a small, mirthless laugh. "Oh, I doubt it! But thank you for saying so."

"Listen to me, Stephanie." He caught her chin, made her look him straight in the eye. "You are exactly as a woman should be, and I am glad I found you again. But you're right when you say not everything remains the same as it once was."

Her gaze grew dark and wary. Haunted, almost. "I am?"

"*Sì*. I am different. What we just shared was different." He punched lightly at his chest. "I felt it here. We were more *di forti sentimenti* with each other. We shared more...*promessa.*'' He tilted her face up to his. *"Capisce?"*

"Yes. But it doesn't change the past."

"So what does that matter? As long as we agree to let go of old resentments and unhappiness, we can shape a better future."

"Just like that?" she said wryly.

"But yes, just like that!"

"With me sneaking out to meet you every night for the next two weeks?" She squirmed and looked away again. "It doesn't sound so very different to me, Matteo, except that, at the end, I'll be the one to leave, instead of you."

He slid an arm over her hip and pulled her close. Forced her again to meet his gaze. "No more sneaking, *cara*. We are of an age to do as we please, regardless of what your family might have to say."

"But I'm living in the same house with them. I can't flaunt an affair in their faces. It would defeat the whole purpose of our spending the summer together."

"Then come away with me for a week. Give us the chance to find out if what we feel for one another *this* time is made of sterner stuff than what we had before."

"And what about Simon?"

"We'll bring him with us, if you wish."

"To witness his mother sleeping with a stranger? I don't think so!"

"Rediscovering one another amounts to more than just making love, Stephanie! Sex between us has always been good. What we've never had, and very much need, is the luxury of time, of hours at a stretch without outside interference, for us to explore the wider possibilities of our relationship."

Still, she hesitated, and he had to bite back the accusation springing to his lips: *what is it? You need to ask Daddy's permission?*

"Don't look at me like that!" she said, reading his thoughts. You know the only reason I'm in Italy is to honor my grandmother's request that all of us—my father and mother, my brothers and me—try to strengthen our family bond."

"And you seriously think that will ever happen between you and your father or the older brother?"

"Is there any reason it shouldn't?"

"From what I witnessed at lunch today, every reason in the world, *cara mia!* Victor is your father's *burattino*—how do you say it in English?" He jerked his fingers up and down, pulling imaginary strings. "His puppet, yes? *Padre* says 'jump,' and Victor says, 'how high?'

"I'm not Victor!"

"But you spent the first nineteen years of your life trying without success to please your father. That you're here now, still battling the same demon, tells me you've yet to succeed. Do you really expect another few weeks is going to change that?"

"That's not the point. I have to make the effort. Family means everything to my grandparents."

"It means everything to me, too, Stephanie. To have children, to watch a son take his first, unsteady steps into my outstretched arms, to have a baby daughter wrap her tiny fist around my finger, to feel my heart swell with love and pride for them…these, when they happen, will be my most prized accomplishments."

She flinched as if he'd struck her, and again a haunted misery flickered in her lovely blue eyes. *"Don't!"* she begged.

He caught her face between his palms. "Tell me what troubles you so deeply, *cara*. Because it has to do with more than honoring your promise to *Signora* Anna. I know in my bones that there is more."

A tear rolled down her cheek, then another. And sud-

denly he remembered what she'd said just a moment before. *It's got nothing to do with my father—at least not
in the way you think....*

"Tell me!" he said urgently, an unspeakably ugly suspicion assailing him. "Did your father...?" He stopped,
choking over the word begging to be aired. But her wide,
terrified gaze drove him on. "Did he abuse you? Or no,
not him, but your brother Victor? Was he the one?
Because if so, I will kill him!"

"No!" she cried, curling up into a ball. "Nothing dis-
gusting like that! It's...it's my grandfather. He's a very
sick man and this is probably the last summer he'll be
with us. He's the reason I can't bail on my promise to
stay here."

"So that's it!" Relief and sorrow swept over him in
equal measure and he cradled her against him as if she
were a child. "Ah, Stephanie, that such a fine man should
have to bribe his children to love one another is tragic."

"Then you do understand?"

"*Sì*. And I admire your devotion, your willingness to
fulfill his wish. Just don't reject my invitation out of hand,
because I don't believe he would want you to turn away
from the chance to find greater happiness. We've been
given a gift, my Stephanie—a small window of opportunity, as they like to say in your country. If there is any
way to take advantage of it ...."

He left the sentence hanging, knowing he'd done all he
could, and the rest was up to her.

She looked at him pensively. "Even if I were to agree
to come away with you, I couldn't be gone a whole week.
It wouldn't be fair, not to Simon or my grandparents."

"Then we'll make it a day or two only," he said, recognizing a shift in her thinking. "Just long enough for
you to learn something about the man I really am, and
for us then to decide if we want to pursue this relationship

after your time here comes to an end. I'm not suggesting we swear lasting commitment to each other on such short notice, only that we leave ourselves open to the possibility.''

Again she hesitated, but this time he saw longing in her eyes. "Let me think about it.''

"That's all I ask.'' He dropped a kiss on her mouth.

Not a smart move! Their lips clung. Lingered. She closed her eyes; caressed his face. One touch, and the dying sparks of spent passion caught fire again.

He wanted to imprint the taste of her in his memory; the feel of her smoother-than-cream skin, the scent of her hair. But night had slipped into early morning and he wasn't willing to settle for another hasty, hungry joining of bodies, with worry gnawing at the back of her mind because she'd stayed away from her son for too long.

When...*if* they made love again, it would be with the full realization on both their parts that they were taking a major step forward in their long journey of discovery.

So, "Stop tormenting me,'' he growled, reluctantly dragging himself out of bed and stepping into his shorts. "It's time I took you home.''

She popped upright, the sheet clutched to her breasts, and peered at the clock on the nightstand. "I had no idea it was so late! I told my mother I wouldn't be away very long, and I've been here over two hours. Hand me my clothes, will you?''

He retrieved her dress and underpants, found her other shoe, and laughed when she blushed and said, "Turn your back, Matteo. You're not going to watch me getting dressed.''

Bewitched by the contradictions he saw in her—demure and innocent on the one hand, sophisticated and provocative on the other—he smiled and said, "I'll wait for you downstairs, then walk you back to the villa.''

She shook her head. "No, better not. I'll be fine on my own."

He didn't want to let her go. Nor did he understand how, when he'd been so certain there was nothing left between them, he could have fallen so quickly and completely under her spell. He did know it had to do with more than sex.

Could it possibly be love? Was this deep, stirring need to cherish and protect a woman what made the difference between passing attraction and lasting commitment? Time would tell.

He went with her as far as the courtyard gate. When she was safely on the other side, she shook his hand, an absurd yet oddly touching gesture in light of the intimacy they'd so recently shared. "Good night, Matteo. Thank you for…everything."

"Good night, Stephanie," he replied soberly. "I'll wait to hear from you. The next move's yours."

The minute she passed beyond his magnetic field, her appalling lapse in judgment and self-control made its presence felt in an overwhelming tide of regret, and she cursed under her breath.

Make the next move? Go away with him? Was she *crazy,* even to consider the suggestion?

Don't worry, you won't get pregnant, he'd said, brandishing his condom as if it were some sort of talisman capable of warding off all disaster. Ha! Little he knew! Condoms sometimes failed. Simon was living proof of that! And even when they didn't, they offered no protection against a broken heart.

So how foolish did that make her, that she'd allowed him to seduce her yet again?

Still berating herself, she slipped quietly back through the gardens and let herself into the villa. At least no one was waiting up, to see what time she came home. The last thing she needed was another confrontation. One a night was enough!

Once in her own room, she debated taking a bath or shower, but feared the sound of running water might betray her late return. So she slid between the sheets of her own bed, the scent of Matteo, of love, still clinging to her body, and turned out the light—another in her long list of mistakes where he was concerned!

The instant the room plunged into darkness, her mind lit up with Technicolor pictures of his lovemaking. Her flesh puckered and sang as it relived his touch. Images of him, naked and powerful, stormed her senses: the solid planes of muscle underlying the warm smooth texture of his skin; the silken weight of his arousal; the taste of him, of herself, when he brought his mouth to hers; the hypnotic seduction of his voice, heavily accented, irresistibly attractive.

Oh, honestly! This was sheer self-indulgence and she wouldn't allow it! Snapping on the lamp again, she concentrated instead on the room's soothing ivory walls, the graceful Italian provincial furniture, the bouquet of flowers beside her bed. They lessened Matteo's sensory onslaught on her body, but did nothing to dispel his vastly more dangerous impact on her heart.

He'd said he wasn't the same man he used to be and she realized shakily that he was right. The Matteo she'd once known hadn't been given to gentle persuasion. His had been a take-it-or-leave-it attitude, and when she hadn't been able to meet his uncompromising expectations, *he'd* left *her*—high and dry, and pregnant.

He'd never been open to discussion; never ended an evening with *Think about it. The next move's up to you.* Never, for that matter, had he once implied they might have a future together. Instead, he'd made it plain theirs was a summer affair, and if she'd fallen in love with him anyway, it was her own damn fault. She'd known from the outset what the rules were.

Tonight, though, he'd been tender, patient, kind.

Matteo *kind?*

She'd have laughed aloud if the idea hadn't unnerved her so. *Sexy, devil-may-care and chauvinistic* might have applied, but *kind* had never once entered the equation! That it crept in now, changed everything. She'd been girlishly infatuated, bewitched and bedazzled by the old Matteo. But this new model...oh, him she could learn to love as only a woman knew how. Deeply. Irrevocably.

Enough to trust him again with her heart.

Enough to trust him with her son's.

But not, sadly, enough to tell him the truth.

"Did you enjoy yourself last night?" her mother wanted to know, when Stephanie staggered down to breakfast the next morning, hollow-eyed from lack of sleep.

"Yes, thank you," she said, fully aware of her grandmother observing her with bright, birdlike curiosity. "I had a very...nice time."

Nice, dearie? How about, so amazing that it's taking everything you've got not to race back over to Matteo's place and beg for a repeat performance!

"I'm so pleased," Vivienne said, her smile wistful. "You should take time for yourself more often, Stephanie. Simon wasn't a speck of trouble, and I'd be happy to look after him again."

"I don't expect I'll ask you to do that, Mom, but thanks for the offer."

As the day wore on, though, and she found herself drifting through it, so preoccupied with thoughts of Matteo that she was barely aware of her surroundings, temptation eroded her resolve. She told herself she needed to see him again, not to leap into bed with him for the momentary release of sex, but to discuss, rationally and calmly, the sheer impracticality of continuing a relationship beset by so many obvious drawbacks. She owed him that much.

"If you're sure you don't mind, perhaps I will go out again tonight," she said, as casually as she knew how, when she joined her mother and grandmother for afternoon tea.

"Good for you!" Vivienne replied. "Distance is so hard on a relationship, especially one in the early stages. You and Matteo need to make the most of the time you have left."

"You know about Matteo and me?" Stephanie's jaw dropped.

"Close your mouth, my love," her grandmother said gently, shooting her a warning glance. "Yes, your mother knows. So would your father, if he bothered to look any further than the end of his aristocratic nose. For what it's worth, your face lights up like a Christmas tree whenever Matteo's name's mentioned."

"It's not quite the way you think," she tried to explain. "We're not really...involved."

Vivienne patted her knee. "You don't have to pretend with us, Stephanie, and you don't have to worry. Your secret's safe. But darling, don't be like me. Don't let your dreams wither and die because you don't have the courage to make them come true."

"I've never heard you talk like this before, Mother!"

"Because I've always been more concerned with keeping the peace at any price. It's only recently that I've seen it's costing me more than it's worth. If you don't fight for what you want, Stephanie, no one else will, and you *will* end up like me: too old to do anything about it.''

''As long as you have breath in your body, you're never too old, Vivienne,'' her mother-in-law said briskly. ''Bruce has become lazy and complacent, but he wasn't always this way and you have to take some of the blame for that. You've been too willing to let him ride rough-shod over you. Perhaps if you'd set a better example, Stephanie wouldn't be reduced to conducting her love affair in secret now.''

''It's hardly a love affair, Grandmother!'' Stephanie protested.

''Call it what you like, darling girl, but I ought to recognize the symptoms when I see them. Your grandfather and I have been engaged in a love affair that's lasted nearly seventy years. Are you going to be able to say the same, when you get to be my age?''

Probably, at the rate she was going! The difference was, she'd be the only one who knew it. Matteo had lived in her heart for the past ten years and, if the state she was in now was any indication, he'd continue to do so for the rest of her natural life.

She might as well face it. The pain of loving him, which had subsided over time into a dull ache, had come roaring back with a vengeance, a raging monster of need which consumed her every waking second.

She longed to be with him, to listen to him, look at him, touch him, lose herself in his arms, welcome him into her body, share his thoughts, his ideas, his dreams…the list was endless. Too bad all her wanting was poisoned with a fear that prevented her from making the most of it when opportunity came knocking.

''So *will* you go out again tonight, then?'' Her mother regarded her archly.

She pursed her lips. Debated the point. And knew that however strongly her rational self might say otherwise, there was only one possible reply. "Yes," she said. "I'll go out again tonight."

To see him one last time. To explain that they could have no future. To find closure in saying goodbye.

Good reasons, every one. *Sensible* reasons.

CHAPTER EIGHT

SHE realized at once that he'd been expecting her. A kerosene lantern shone by the courtyard gate. There were candles burning in the living room, and wine chilling in a marble cooler on the coffee table. He'd even dressed for the occasion and, instead of casual shorts, wore a pair of tailored linen pants and a white cotton shirt whose turned-back sleeves contrasted sharply against his deeply tanned forearms.

"I'm glad you came," he said, meeting her at the front door.

"I'm here only to talk," she informed him.

He took her in his arms. "Of course."

The too-familiar exhilaration streamed through her blood, leaving her desperate for his kiss. Blind with yearning, she wriggled free. "I mean it, Matteo," she said breathlessly. "I really just want to talk."

"About?"

"Us, and the reason we can't carry on like this."

"Like what, precisely?"

"*This* for a start!" She flapped her hand between them. "Glomming onto one another like a couple of horn dogs, every chance we get."

"Horn dogs?" His dark, level brows rose in silent reproof. "That's how you define our lovemaking?"

"Not...exactly."

"Then how, exactly?"

"Well, it's been very nice, but—"

"*Nice?*" The word exploded from his mouth.

"More than nice," she amended hurriedly. "I'll be

honest with you, Matteo. It would be very easy for me to fall into bed with you again tonight. But I'm not going to, because it wouldn't be sensible.''

''Sensible?'' He stared at her as if she'd suddenly grown two heads. ''Stephanie, *cara,* shoes are sensible. Wise investments are sensible. Proper diet and exercise are sensible. But I had no idea making love fell into that category. I've always seen it as memorable, enjoyable, and even, on occasion, incomparable. But the day—or night—I start regarding it as *sensible,* I'll check myself into the nearest monastery and take lifelong vows of chastity.''

''Perhaps 'sensible' wasn't the best word choice,'' she said, squirming under his uncompromising scrutiny. ''Perhaps what I should have said is 'advisable.' It is not *advisable* for us to engage in sexual intimacy.''

For a moment, he continued to stare at her. Then he started to shake. His white shirt rippled across his chest as if blown by an invisible breeze. And then the laughter came pouring out, deep and rich and so infectious that she smiled despite herself.

''I'm not trying to be funny, Matteo,'' she said, quickly bringing herself under control.

''Then God help me when you are!''

He was much too irresistible when he laughed, and she wished he'd stop. ''No, really!'' she said severely. ''It's unrealistic to think we can bridge a decade-long gap in communication by rushing into bed.''

Sobering, he said, ''Then how do you suggest we do it?''

''That's my whole point. We can't. It might be different if we lived close to one another and could take things slowly.''

''And sensibly.''

"Yes," she said, defiantly. "Mock me all you like, but there's nothing wrong with being sensible sometimes."

"I agree, Stephanie. You're absolutely right."

"It's really for the best to end things now, before either of us gets in too deep."

"Indeed, yes!" he agreed, mercifully choosing not to make much of who was getting in where too deep.

"We went ten years without exchanging a word, after all," she pointed out righteously, "then in the space of a few days, we forgot all the reasons we didn't work out the first time around, and picked right up where we'd left off."

"Exactly."

"At our age, there's no excuse for repeating mistakes."

"None at all."

"We're supposed to learn from them."

"*Sì.*"

"Well, there you are, then. Now that we've cleared the air, we can close the door on the past and part as friends."

"Can we?" he said, his expression veiled. "Who are you trying to convince, Stephanie? Me, or yourself?"

"Well, you, of course!"

"But you didn't have to come here to do that. I made it very clear, yesterday, that the next move was up to you, so all you had to do, today, was nothing. I'd have got the message."

"I thought it only fair to speak to you face-to-face."

"*D'accordo!* Okay! You've accomplished what you came to do." He placed his hand in the small of her back, pivoted her around, and swept her unceremoniously out into the courtyard. "*Grazie, buona fortuna, e buona notte!*"

Miserable in victory, she stumbled as far as the gate. Willed herself not to look back, to keep her reluctant feet moving.

Moving *away* from him.

And could do neither.

"Is there a problem, Stephanie?"

She turned and filled her starving gaze with the sight of him. He leaned in the doorway, one broad shoulder propped against the side of the frame, one long leg braced at the ankle across the other, the thumb of one hand hooked in the pocket of his narrow-fitting pants.

"Yes," she whimpered pathetically. "It's the same as it was last night. I don't really want to go."

The next afternoon, Corinna showed up at the villa. She had on a white peasant blouse, and a full, swirling skirt strewn with scarlet hibiscus and royal blue cornflowers. Toenails flawlessly lacquered to match her fingernails peeped from her straw sandals, and she carried a straw bag with a freshly cut hibiscus bloom pinned to the side.

"I came to see you," she told Stephanie, when Vivienne suggested she join them for afternoon tea. "Is there some place we can talk in private? The gazebo, perhaps?"

She led the way into the garden without waiting for an answer and Stephanie, who until then had been floating on a cloud of pure bliss, followed, filled with a sense of foreboding that left her clammy with trepidation.

"So," Corinna began without preamble, perching gracefully beside her on a white-enameled bench, a gorgeous, exotic butterfly keeping company with a thoroughly unremarkable moth, "you and Matteo have been spending time together, *sì?*"

Although technically the guest and therefore under some obligation to defer to the wishes of her hostess, her poise and self-command were such that she exuded an air of unshakable authority. In a contest of wills, there was little doubt about who'd emerge the winner.

It wasn't fair for one woman to be so overwhelmingly beautiful and completely invincible, Stephanie thought, feeling downright anemic in her pale green sundress. "Some," she admitted, wishing she'd taken time to blow-dry her hair after swimming with Simon, instead of scooping it haphazardly into a knot on top of her head.

"And you like him?" Corinna cast a knowing glance at her. "You like Matteo very much?"

What was the point in denying the obvious? "Yes."

"Enough not to hurt him?"

"Yes," she said again, puzzled. "What makes you think otherwise?"

Ignoring the question, Corinna said, "He tells me you're going away together for the weekend. That you're leaving tomorrow afternoon for his home in Tuscany, and not returning until Monday morning."

"That's right." Suddenly feeling as if she were eighteen again, and subject to being treated as someone not quite in command of all her faculties, Stephanie returned Corinna's gaze in full measure and said boldly, "What's all this leading up to, Corinna? Are you jealous?"

Corinna's reaction was startling, to say the least. Dropping her bag on the floor, she clasped her hands in her lap and, closing her eyes, laid her head against the high back of the bench. "Oh, I am jealous indeed!" she sighed. "I am jealous of your youth, Stephanie."

Stephanie waited, uncertain how to respond, or even if a response was expected. That this command performance had to do with Matteo had never been in question, but perhaps not, she was beginning to think, quite in the way she'd first supposed.

After a moment, Corinna continued, "If I were younger, I would marry him in a flash, were he to ask me. But I'm forty-eight, well past child-bearing age, and Matteo deserves a wife who can give him a son." She opened her eyes then, and without moving her head, slid her amber gaze sideways to connect with Stephanie's. "Do you not agree that he deserves a son, Stephanie? That it would be a crime to deny him that right?"

Stephanie's mouth ran dry and her heart thudded to a stop, before lurching to life again. With crystal clarity she recalled Corinna's searching examination of Simon the day she'd met him, and her oddly cryptic remarks.

… *Cosi biondo…cosi familiare…he could pass for an Italian with such skin….*

"If there's a point to all this," Stephanie said, horribly afraid that there was, "I'm afraid I'm missing it."

Corinna reached into her bag, withdrew what appeared to be a folded embossed card stippled brown and yellow with age in places, and passed it to Stephanie. "Does this help you find it, *cara?*"

Unwillingly, Stephanie opened it, and felt the blood drain down into her ankles at what she discovered. Inside was a photograph of Simon when he'd been about eighteen months old. Except it couldn't be Simon. Everything about it—the era in which it was taken, the sepia tint, *everything* was wrong!

This child, who looked out with Simon's wide-set eyes and smiled at the camera with Simon's sweet little boy dimples, wore a long dress trimmed with fine lace, and had a ribbon in her short, blond hair. But take away the unfamiliar background, the obvious disparity in time, and she could have been his twin. To pretend otherwise was futile. The resemblance was indisputable.

Stephanie's hands began to shake. "Where did you get this?" she asked in a shell-shocked whisper.

"From an album of old photographs I discovered in my house about a year ago. They were in a trunk, along with memorabilia from the Second World War. It took me a while to find this particular print, but I made the connection the day you came to lunch. You're looking now at a picture of Matteo's paternal grandmother.''

"I don't believe you! Matteo looks nothing like her."

"No, he takes after the Italian side of the family. But she was Swiss. Blond and blue-eyed. Just like your Simon. An extraordinary coincidence, wouldn't you say?''

What *could* she say? The truth had come out in a way she'd never anticipated, and there was no stuffing it back into secrecy. Numb with dread, she stared at Corinna and asked hollowly, "What are you going to do about it?''

"Are you admitting that Simon is Matteo's son?''

Stripped of energy, tired of lying, and painted into a corner entirely of her own making, Stephanie wilted on the bench. "You haven't left me much choice, have you?''

"Then the question, my dear, is what are *you* going to do? One way or another, Matteo *will* learn the truth, of that you may be sure. But I suggest it would sound better coming from you.''

"How, Corinna?" she burst out wretchedly, tears welling up in her eyes. "You appear to have all the answers before I even know there's a question, so tell me, how do I do that without destroying what he and I are on the brink of rediscovering with one another? Or is that what you're hoping for—that he'll walk away from me, and you'll have him all to yourself again?''

Corinna retrieved the photo and took firm hold of Stephanie's trembling hands. "Listen to me, *cara*," she said kindly. "I am not your enemy, nor do I have any wish to come between you and Matteo.''

"But you'll do it anyway!''

"If I must, yes." She sighed again, and gave Stephanie's hands a last squeeze before releasing them. "Despite what you appear to think, I like you, Stephanie.

I feel for you at this most difficult time, and I don't pretend that the task facing you will be easy. But if you force me to choose sides, I will choose Matteo's. He and I have known each other from the time we were children spending our summers here on Ischia. My primary loyalty lies with him. I know how deeply he reveres family, how much he hopes to have one of his own someday. Please don't ask me to betray him by hiding the truth about this child he fathered.''

''But we've only just found each other again!'' Stephanie protested, seeing all her newly-minted dreams evaporating. ''We're just beginning to rebuild our relationship!''

Producing a handkerchief, Corinna dabbed gently at Stephanie's cheeks. ''Do you love him, my dear?''

''Yes,'' she sobbed. ''I've always loved him.''

''Enough to forgive him, if he were to tell you he'd fathered a child by another woman?''

Did she? Heavy-hearted, Stephanie turned away, knowing the answer and wishing she could refute it. But what use trying to fool Corinna, if she couldn't fool herself? ''There's nothing he could do or say that I wouldn't forgive.''

''Then trust him to be equally generous. Matteo is a good man, a fair man.''

That much she knew to be true. Maturity had softened his hard edges, endowed him with compassion and humanity. But he was no saint. There was a limit to what he'd tolerate, and no amount of sweet reason could mitigate the enormity of her deception.

''Oh!'' she cried, beside herself. ''If you had to ruin my life, couldn't you have waited a few more days and let me have this one, perfect weekend with him, first?''

''It's because you do have this weekend that I spoke when I did. Think about it, Stephanie! This way, you'll have uninterrupted time together to work things out. There'll be no running away from the truth by either of you."

"I'll spoil everything. He'll be so angry!"

"*Sì, furioso*. But he will also be *grato*—grateful for the gift you bring to him. Simon is a beautiful child. What man would not welcome him as a son?" Again, she reached for Stephanie's hands and shook them gently. "Have faith, *cara!* Believe in Matteo."

An hour ago, she had. But an hour ago, she'd still been high on memories of the night before....

"I don't really want to go," she'd confessed when, despite her every intention, she hadn't been able to open the gate and walk away from him.

"Then stay. Stop all this nonsense and come here."

He'd held open his arms, and she'd flown into them. Buried her face against his neck and drawn in the warm, intoxicating man-scent of him. "You must think I'm such a fool."

"No," he murmured. "*Al contrario, cara mia,* I understand you better than you think."

"But I don't understand myself." She leaned back, the better to search his face, and fanned her fingers over her breast. "Matteo, I don't understand what's happening here! I'm not a teenager anymore. I ought to be able to control myself. And I do, when I'm not with you. I tell myself I won't let you sweep me off my feet again, that nothing good can come of this. But as soon as we're together, the wanting comes back, and it's as you said last night: it's not just about sex anymore."

"No," he said huskily. "It's about two people who lost each other many years ago, and by some miracle have the chance to find their way back to one another. That's why I asked you to come away with me—so that we can embark together on the long journey from yesterday to today.''

"And I—"

He silenced her with a short, hard kiss. "I know. You promised this time to your grandparents."

"That's not what I was going to say!"

"No?"

"No. My father and Victor plan to spend the weekend in Capri, and Drew's flying to Rome to visit a college friend. So, if the invitation still stands, this would be the perfect time for you and me to get away also."

"Your grandparents won't mind?"

"Not a bit. They'd never come out and say so, of course, but I think they're finding having six people underfoot all the time a lot more tiring than they'd expected, and they're quite looking forward to a bit of peace and quiet."

"What can I say then, except that, for once, I'm grateful to your father?"

Undone by his slow smile, by the promise she saw in his dark eyes, she said, "You could tell me you want to make love to me again."

"I have to say the words?" He cradled her bottom and pulled her hips playfully against his, against the prominent contour of his arousal glaringly evident through the snug fit of his linen pants. "You can't figure out for yourself that I'm more than ready, more than willing, to do exactly that?"

"Talk's cheap," she said, lowering her gaze in a parody of prim modesty. "Show me the proof."

His low laughter grazed her mouth, sent a thrill of anticipation racing along her nerves. "Then come with me, my love," he growled, lifting her effortlessly into his arms, "and I'll supply all the proof you could possibly ask for."

Although the corners of his bedroom lay draped in shadows, the moon splashed bright silver coins of light through the open window. Enough for him to find the buttons down the front of her blouse. Enough for her to see the impassioned rise and fall of his chest.

He turned undressing her into a ritual of worship, unhurriedly removing each item of her clothing and pausing to admire with a word, a brief, tormenting caress, each inch of skin he exposed. "This place here...and here... and here," he murmured, pressing hot, damp kisses at the base of her throat, the hollow of her shoulder, the slope of her breast, "taste of peaches kissed by the sun."

All that lovely attention she'd accepted with some degree of equanimity, filing away in her memory for later pleasure each erotic touch, every tender word. But when he sank down and buried his tongue between her thighs, the meltdown effect was so total that her mind went dark, her knees buckled, and she swayed against him.

From somewhere deep within her, a wild, primitive sound erupted. She clutched handfuls of his hair, raked her nails over his shoulders.

It was too much—*he* was too much! "No more!" she begged brokenly, when at last the mists cleared and she could speak coherently again. "Let me undress you now! I want to feel all of you against me, skin to skin."

He rose to his feet, accepting with tortured patience her fumbling attempts to unbuckle his belt and draw down the zipper at his fly, and pull his shirt free and tear open its buttons, and oh, to possess him as he'd possessed her! To run her palms at leisure over the crisp dusting of hair on his chest and follow its path as it narrowed down his torso in a long, dark stripe. To cradle his taut buttocks and pull him just close enough for the smooth, silken tip of his penis to brush questingly against her.

She loved touching him. Loved the hard, heated texture

of him, the underlying strength, the sculpted shape. After so many years of making do with recycled memories, she delighted in the solid flesh and blood reality of him.

"You are killing me!" he groaned, when she took her fingertip and traced a delicate heart over his groin, then dipped her head and stroked her tongue over the thick, heavy weight of him. "And you've gone unpunished long enough."

The vengeance he wreaked left her dazed and delirious. In a heartbeat, he had her stretched out beneath him on the bed. She felt cool sheets at her back, and thought that they must be freshly laundered because she could smell lavender.

Then she stopped thinking altogether because he was inflicting such relentless bliss to her body again that even the soles of her feet puckered with delight. Finally, in a quiet, almost exploratory way, he entered her. Not very far. Just enough to leave her screaming silently for more.

Opening her eyes, she found him staring down at her, his expression somber, his gaze locked unblinkingly with hers. A pulse throbbed at his temple and she could feel his heart knocking at his ribs. Otherwise, he remained motionless.

At length, he moved again. An abbreviated thrust only. A taste of heaven too soon withdrawn.

The darkest recesses of her body clutched and convulsed. She opened her mouth to beg, but he silenced her with his tongue, plunging it deep into her mouth at the same time that he drove hard into her. And then, the race was on.

His hips ground against hers in frantic rhythm. The bed rocked and groaned in sympathy as she fought the encroaching climax. She wanted to remain clear-headed, to capture for eternity this night, this moment, in all its perfection.

She wanted the impossible! Nothing could survive the earth-shattering force of the ecstasy which burst over her like a thousand shimmering stars. Nothing could halt the towering magnificence of his ultimate surrender.

But later, in the close union of heart and soul only ever found after two people have made love, but never present when all they've had is sex, she found it *was* possible to improve on perfection. Because, as she lay with her head on his chest and his hand lazily stroking her back, he said ruefully, "Are men in general more *stupido* than women, or am I unique in not having seen until now what's been staring me in the face all along?"

"And what's that?" she asked, hearing the tenderness in his voice, but afraid to read more into his actual words than he intended.

"That we belong together," he said. "That I've been in love with you from the beginning, and neither time nor distance has changed that."

She'd thought her heart would shatter with joy, and if the niggling voice of conscience had tried to spoil the moment by warning her that *nothing* was sacred or perfect as long as deception was part of the mix, she'd shut it out. Tonight belonged to her and Matteo, and only them. There'd be time enough later to deal with the rest.

She just hadn't planned on "later" happening quite so soon or with such unnerving brutality.

Eyes streaming, she turned again to Corinna, "Let me have just one perfect weekend with him," she implored. "Please, Corinna, don't take that away from me. Matteo and I need to cement our relationship. It's too new to withstand such a shock so soon."

"Do you really think you'll be able to hide from him the fact that you're deeply troubled by what's waiting for you, when you come back? Will you be able to lie in his arms and return his kisses without flinching? Or will guilt make you turn away from the candor you find in his eyes? Will it paralyze you to the point that you cannot respond to his lovemaking? And if all those things come to pass, what kind of memories will either of you bring away, when your 'perfect' weekend is over?''

The truth battered Stephanie on every side. She wanted to hate this beautiful widow who touched her arm with such compassion. Wanted to shut out that kind, wise voice. Wished she could attribute Corinna's advice to self-interest, a malicious tearing down of another woman's idyll because her own had gone unfulfilled.

She could do none of those things. Instead, she buried her face in her hands and sobbed aloud. She might have deceived Matteo, but there was a limit to how much she could deceive herself.

"Stephanie, *cara!*" Corinna folded her in her arms. "Come, this must stop. You'll make yourself ill."

Ill? It felt more like dying—the death of the one dream she'd never thought would come true but which, for too brief a time, had hung within reach.

Corinna stood, pulled Stephanie to her feet also, and said firmly, "I'm taking you home."

"No!" Simon couldn't see her like this. No one could.

"To my house. To give you time to compose yourself before you face your family again. Don't worry that we'll meet Matteo. He's gone to *Ischia Porto* to finalize arrangements for your trip to Tuscany."

Barely conscious of the sun blazing down, filling the air with the thick, sweet scent of flowers and turning the sea into a blinding sheet of diamond-flecked blue silk, Stephanie allowed herself to be led away. Even Guido the parrot's raucous welcome seemed to echo from a great distance.

"Come!" Slipping an arm around her waist, Corinna

steered her across the terrace and into the villa, to a pow-
der room at the end of a long central hall. "Wash your
face, *cara,* and I will order us some refreshment," she
said, before quietly closing the door.

Stephanie sagged against the marble vanity and stared
in horror at the ravaged image confronting her in the mirror. Eyes swollen half shut and tinted red to match her
nose, she looked more like a deranged pig than a human
being. It would take more than a splash of cold water to
repair this much damage.

Corinna was obviously of the same opinion. "You need
help," she determined, observing Stephanie critically
when they two of them were seated in a salon shaded from
the outside heat by louvered blinds. "It's as well I had
Baptiste prepare cucumber slices. They are good for re-
ducing swelling around the eyes. Rest your head against
the cushions, and let's get to work."

Aware of the irony implicit in the scene, Stephanie
asked, "Why are you being so good to me?"

"Because you are a good person who made a mistake,"
Corinna said, patting the cucumber in place. "And because Matteo loves you."

Stephanie's heart fluttered with feeble hope. That he'd
said as much to her the night before, in the afterglow of
passion, didn't carry nearly the same weight as if he'd
admitted it to Corinna when he was at his most rational.
"Did he tell you that?"

"Not in so many words. But I know him well, and I
see how he looks at you."

A consoling enough remark but, like the wafer-thin cucumber slices soothing her eyes, it offered brief respite
only. "I doubt he'll look at me quite the same way, after
I tell him about Simon."

"Do you intend bringing your son with you tomorrow?"

"I considered it, but my mother gets to spend time with him so seldom that she asked me to leave him with her, and I'm glad, now, that I agreed. I don't think it'd help any, having to worry about him overhearing Matteo tearing strips off me."

"Matteo might surprise you. He's made his share of mistakes, too, you know."

"I suppose so. But never one as grievous as mine." She sighed at the gloomy uncertainty awaiting her. This morning, she'd hardly been able to wait for tomorrow to come. Now she dreaded its arrival. If only she could glean some insight to how he might react, how best to broach the subject. "Tell me about the years since I first met him, Corinna," she begged. "Help me understand what's made him the man he is today."

Corinna's answer was guarded and long in coming. "I can't fill in the lost years, Stephanie. That's for you and Matteo to do, together. I can tell you that he's a complicated man, that he's proud and stubborn. But I think you know these things already.

"As for what you don't know…my best advice is, make the most of these four days and three nights. Don't waste a single moment of the opportunity they bring. Above all, don't wait until the last minute to tell him about his son. Get it out of the way early, and give yourselves the rest of the time to deal with the repercussions."

CHAPTER NINE

SHE'D thought they'd probably fly to Tuscany, given that Matteo had told her their destination lay a good three hundred miles north of Ischia, but not for a minute had Stephanie expected they'd travel by private helicopter or that he'd pilot it himself. How many more surprises did he have in store?

"Nervous?" he inquired, adjusting his headset and smiling at her white-knuckled grip on the padded arms of her seat as the craft lifted off.

"A little."

"Never flown in one of these before?"

She shook her head, and clenched her teeth on a hissed intake of breath as the Bell JetRanger tilted away from the island and headed north over the Tyrrhenian Sea.

He reached across and covered her knee. "Relax, Stephanie. You're in safe hands."

"I'm sure," she said, "but while we're in the air, I'd feel a whole lot better if you kept them both on the controls."

He laughed. "I've been flying for seven years and never come close to an accident. I know enough not to take chances. And this is a top-of-the-line helicopter. Corinna's late husband bought it, just before he died, and he never settled for anything but the best. Sit back and enjoy the scenery, *tesoro*. I promise we'll be landing safe and sound in less than two hours, just in time for sunset."

"Landing where, exactly?" She ventured a glance below. As far as the eye could see, the Italian coastline unwound, ribbon-like, along the edge of the cobalt-blue wa-

129

ter. "Tuscany covers a pretty wide area, and you've never mentioned a precise location. Are we going to Florence?"

"You'd like that?"

Her blood quickened. Florence, rich in art treasures, appealed to the romantic in her and was one of the cities on her must-see list, once Simon was a little older. "Very much. I've read so much about it."

"Then I'm sorry to disappoint you, because I'm taking you instead to Lucca, where I was born. It's a little mediaeval town, not as fashionably popular with tourists as *Firenze*, but a real gem with wonderful architecture, and hardly any traffic to speak of within its walls. We can walk or cycle everywhere, and when I've shown you all there is to see of the town itself, I'll drive you into the hills to the wineries and olive oil mills."

"It sounds heavenly."

"It is. If we were staying longer, I'd take you to *Firenze* also, but it's an hour's drive away and deserves to be explored at leisure, so we'll save it for the next time."

She didn't tell him there likely wouldn't be a next time, because that would have begged the question *why not?* And despite Corinna's advice to tell Matteo as soon as possible that he was Simon's father, conveying such life-altering secrets to a man at the controls of a helicopter, flying several hundred feet over open sea, didn't strike Stephanie as the most propitious time in which to do so.

Instead, gesturing at the well-appointed interior of the machine, she said, "Is flying this thing job-related, or do you do it for pleasure?"

"Mostly for work. It enables me to get from Carrara to Ischia quickly."

"And Corinna doesn't mind?"

"Why would she?"

"Well, you live in her gardener's cottage, so I assume

that means you work for her part of the time. And since this is her helicopter...."

His laughter this time was underscored with something she couldn't quite identify—irony, perhaps, or mockery? "You really don't know much about me, do you, Stephanie?"

"No," she said, wishing she could see the expression in his eyes. But even when he flung her a glance, the only thing looking back at her was her own twin reflection in his aviator sunglasses. "And at the risk of repeating myself *ad nauseam,* I've been trying to make that point with you, ever since we...hooked up again. Outside the bedroom, we're virtual strangers. It's not just that we've lived distant lives, this past ten years, which is a long time by anyone's standards—"

"Then what is it?"

She shrugged, the enormous task of bridging those lost years in four short days, of expecting him to understand the choices she'd made, seeming suddenly hopeless. "It's that we never really got to know anything about each other to begin with."

"We knew enough not to be able to keep our hands off one another!"

"And that's about all. We never scratched below the surface." She gave a short, bitter laugh. "You showed up out of the blue, one day, and it never once occurred to me to ask why or how."

"You know why. I came to find out if your grandfather's invention could work at the manufacturing level."

"Yes, but considering Carrara's half a world removed from Bramley Point, Ontario, there had to be more to it than that. Yet I never asked you what it might be. Never asked anything about you personally, or the kind of life you led. All I could think about was the next time I could sneak out of the house to meet you and make love." She eyed him curiously. "How *did* you come to hear about his design? My grandfather was a geologist widely respected in his field, but he never published his research in professional magazines, or anything like that."

"I know, and that's something I've never quite understood. He'd be a millionaire several times over, if he'd patented his ideas."

"He already had money, and didn't care about making more. It was the creative tinkering he enjoyed. So how did news of what he'd done manage to find its way to Italy?"

"Your grandfather and mine met there at the end of World War Two, and struck up a friendship. Although they came from different worlds, they shared a lot in common. Not only were they peaceable men, entirely opposed to the kind of violence war inflicts, they were both in the quarry business, both full of innovative ideas, and just plain liked each other. So they kept in touch, and when my grandfather heard your grandfather had come up with something which could revolutionize the way granite had always been cut, he sent me over to investigate adapting it for use in the marble industry."

"If they were such good friends, why didn't your grandfather come over himself, instead of sending you?"

"He wasn't up to the travel by then. War wounds and failing health kept him close to home." He angled another glance at her, one so loaded with sexual innuendo that even the sunglasses weren't enough to deflect it. "Lucky for me, *sì?* Otherwise, I wouldn't have met you until this summer."

And what a difference it would have made, had that been the case! She'd have wept at such a cruel twist of fate, except how could she regret a past which had given her Simon?

"You haven't mentioned your grandmother," she said,

aware she was venturing onto dangerous ground, but so oppressed by her shameful deceit that she couldn't help herself. "Is she still alive?"

"*Sì.*"

Her heart leaped so violently, she was sure it had flopped loose from its moorings. The aftershock left her quivering all over and every instinct told her to drop the subject *now,* for fear that it land her in trouble she wasn't yet prepared to deal with. But the demons driving her wouldn't allow it. "What's she like?" she asked, in a small voice.

"An older version of my mother."

"Your *mother?*" She stared at him, openmouthed, caught so totally off-guard that she hadn't a hope of hiding her astonishment.

"*Sì!*" His amusement rippled through her headset. "Why does that surprise you?"

As relieved as a convicted murderer being granted a reprieve, she said, "I just assumed you were talking about your father's side of the family."

"Ah, capisco! No, my father's mother died when I was six, so I don't remember her all that well. She and my grandfather moved to Ischia after the war, so they were never as big a factor in my life as my mother's parents. I'd visit the island every summer, right up until my grandfather died eight years ago, but I didn't see much of them in between."

"And your mother's father—the one my grandfather knew?"

Matteo's mouth curved in sudden sorrow. "We lost him just last winter."

She ached to touch him; to let him know with a kiss and a caress that she felt his bereavement as if it were her own. "You were very close, I can tell."

"*Sì,*" he said. "He was more my father than my grandfather, and I very much wish you could have met him. He would have died a happier man knowing that I'd finally found such a woman to love.''

He was ripping out her heart, with no idea that his every word left her bleeding with regret and misery. ''You weren't as close to your real father?''

''During his lifetime, yes. But he was killed on the job when I was just eleven—a bad time in any boy's life to be without a man's guiding influence. And I was a handful, as they say in English. Without my grandfather to keep me in line, I'd have grown up to be nothing but trouble.'' He laughed ruefully. ''Some might say I did, anyway!''

''I don't think so, Matteo. You might have been a hellion in your youth, but you've come a long way since then. Your grandfather must have been proud of you.''

''I hope so. I owe him a great deal.'' His gaze swept the empty sky above and around them, and flicked to the instrument panel. He made some small adjustment to the controls, then settled back in his seat before continuing, ''Your Simon will need just such guidance, Stephanie. The teen years are dangerous for any boy, but especially so in these difficult times.''

She stared fixedly ahead, less because she cared about the view than because she didn't want him to see the sudden surge of tension she was sure must show on her face at the mention of Simon's name. ''I'm fully aware of that,'' she said stiffly

Attributing her chilly response to continued nervousness, Matteo pressed a switch on the control panel, and said, ''A little music might make it easier for you to relax. What's your preference? We've got *Great Opera Choruses,* Chopin's *Nocturnes,* the soundtrack from—''

''Chopin,'' she interrupted, grateful for any legitimate excuse to terminate the conversation. And just to make sure he got the message, she leaned against the back of the club seat's padded headrest, and closed her eyes.

Not for a second did she expect she'd really relax. How could she, knowing what she had to face before the weekend was over? But they weren't called *Nocturnes* for nothing. As the soothing piano recital worked its magic, she felt herself drifting away, if not into a truly deep sleep, then at least into a state of pleasant, dreamlike drowsiness. Even the rhythmic *whoomf, whoomf, whoomf,* of the helicopter blades assumed a lulling cadence. Perhaps the fact that she'd barely slept a wink the night before had something to do with it, too. In any event, when she next became fully conscious of her surroundings, the JetRanger was hovering above a landing pad in the middle of a grassy field bathed in early evening sunshine and swept by the artificial gale created by the machine's whirling rotors.

A moment later, the craft touched down so gently she wouldn't have known they'd landed had Matteo not killed the engine, removed his headphones and sunglasses, and said, "Welcome to Lucca, Stephanie. Didn't I promise to get you here in one piece?"

"Yes. I'm sorry I ever doubted it."

"I make it a point always to keep my promises." He laid his hand against her cheek. "Especially to you, *mi innamorata.*"

He plucked at her heartstrings with such tenderness. *Please don't be so nice to me!* she begged inwardly, turning her face aside and scrunching her eyes shut against the restrained passion she saw in his. *I'm not nearly deserving enough.*

Sensing her distress, he hung up her headset and forced her to look at him. "What is it, Stephanie?" he asked, his voice rough with concern. "Having second thoughts about spending the weekend with me?"

"No," she said, reaching a sudden decision. Morally bound to tell him about his connection to Simon she might be, but why taint their entire time together, as she surely would if she spoke too soon? Didn't it make more sense to lay down a rich tapestry of intimate, special memories first, and hope they'd cushion the inevitable shock of her confession? "Regardless of what happens later, this weekend with you is something I'll neither regret nor forget."

"Then why such shades of sadness? Are you wishing we'd brought Simon with us, after all?"

"No. I miss him, of course, but I really want these few days to be about just you and me." She gestured at the view beyond the helicopter windows, at the backdrop of green hills, and the profusion of towers rising above the ancient walls enclosing the old part of town. "If I seem preoccupied, it's because I'm rather overwhelmed—by the flight here, everything you've told me, the sense of stepping back in time. It's a lot to take in all at once."

"On top of which, it's been a long day and you're probably starving."

"Actually, no. I had a late lunch. But I'm ready to stretch my legs."

"Good thing our ground transportation's arrived, then." He slid open the door and jumped to the ground, just as a low-slung black Ferrari pulled up a few yards away.

After helping her alight, Matteo introduced her to Adriano, the car's driver, who was busily transferring their luggage from the JetRanger's baggage compartment to the Ferrari's trunk.

"*Buona sera, Signora!*" Adriano's smile flashed white in his swarthy face. He was a ruggedly handsome man, somewhere in his mid-fifties, she guessed, with large, capable hands and the strong physique of one used to manual labor.

Ushering her into the car, Matteo called out, "You'll take over from here, Adriano, and have the aircraft ready for take-off Monday morning?"

"*Sì, Signor De Luca*. It will be done." He aimed another smile at Stephanie. "*Buon divertimento, Signora!*"

"What did he say?" she asked Matteo, as they drove away.

"That although he knows you'll make love to me every hour on the hour between now and Monday, he hopes you won't leave me too exhausted to fly us back to Ischia."

On what seemed like the first genuine burst of laughter in days, she said, "He did not!"

"Not in so many words, perhaps, but it amounted to the same. He wished you a good time. Are you very tired, *cara?*"

"Not now that I'm on firm ground again."

He took her hand; held it firmly beneath his as he shifted gears. "Then let's take a tour of the countryside while it's still light. There's something I need to speak about with you."

A thread of uneasiness clutched at her. "You make it sound serious."

"Important, perhaps, but not serious in the way you think." He steered the Ferrari away from the town and up a narrow, twisting road which wound among hillsides washed in the clear, golden light of early evening. Half an hour later—an eternity to Stephanie, during which she braced herself to withstand all sorts of dire revelations—he turned again at a sign marked *Proprietà Privata Vietato L'Accesso!*, and followed a rough, weed-choked track which ended about a mile farther on, on the shores of a small, lonely lake.

Then, as the engine dwindled into silence, he climbed out of the car and held open her door. "Shall we walk awhile?"

"If you like."

He linked her fingers in his and led her down by the water. "You haven't asked where we'll be staying for the next three nights."

Aiming for a lightheartedness she didn't feel, she said, "Are we camping out here?"

"Not that I wouldn't enjoy sharing such an experience with you, but no! My mother and grandmother are hoping we'll stay with them."

"Oh!" She swallowed, more than a little taken aback. "And you think I might not care for the idea because…?"

"Because, in Italy, a man doesn't take a woman home to meet his family unless he harbors very serious intentions toward her. If you're not yet ready to deal with that, Stephanie, you have only to say the word, and I'll arrange for us to stay in a hotel. That was, in fact, my original plan, but when they heard I was bringing you to Lucca, my mother and grandmother both knew you weren't just a casual *qualcuno* passing through my life—here today and gone tomorrow. They knew you had to be important to me in a way no other woman has ever been. And so they begged me to bring you to stay in our home. How do you feel about that?"

How did she feel? Honored. Threatened. Terrified!

Guilt left her throat thick and aching. On the one hand, he was offering her more than she'd ever dared hope for. And he'd probably take it all away again, once he learned the extent to which she'd deceived him.

Would he still want her under his roof, when she told him? Would he ever want her again, at all?

"You hesitate," he murmured, pausing to draw a gentle finger down her cheek. "Have I assumed too much, too soon?"

She shook her head—a fatal mistake because in doing so, she loosed the flood of unshed tears in her eyes, and left them sparkling on her lashes. "No," she gulped. "I'm very touched by your family's generosity."

"You should know that my mother is sixty-six and my grandmother eighty-seven."

"Does that matter?"

"Only insofar as it makes them Italian of the old school." He shot her a rueful glance. "It will mean we must sleep in separate bedrooms."

Not to lie in his arms all night long? Not to make love with him, time after time until they were both sated and then, after a few hours' rest, to awaken and make love yet again?

It shouldn't have mattered. Wouldn't have, if it weren't that such a chance might not come her way again. But, given the circumstances, she cared terribly and he, seeing the disappointment in her eyes and misunderstanding the reason for it, begged, "*Non piangere, tesoro!* Don't cry! We'll find other ways to be together."

He framed her face, followed the tear tracks running down her cheeks with a string of kisses. "Here…now, in this beautiful, isolated place," he whispered against her mouth. "It's ours to enjoy…to enjoy each other. Come with me, Stephanie, over there in the hollow between those rocks…."

Despite her body's sudden craving, she was too North American, too socially repressed not to demur. "No! Someone might see—!"

"No one will see," he said roughly. "This land is posted private property, and people in these parts respect such warning."

"So how come we're here?"

He kissed her again, lingeringly. "Because we're allowed to be. I have special dispensation."

The touch of his lips, and his voice, husky with desire, were all it took to send a ripple of sensation spiking in a hot stream directly from her breasts to between her legs. She clung to him, drinking in the taste and texture of his mouth, wanting to be consumed by him. Without another murmur, she allowed him to lead her to the secluded spot he'd pointed out.

The sun had disappeared but remnants of its dying light flared raspberry red, low across the sky, and its daytime warmth lay embedded in the fine sand nestled between the rocks. Clumps of wildflowers, yellow and purple, dotted the area. The quiet murmur of tiny waves lapping ashore mingled with the sleepy chirp of birds.

If this wasn't the Garden of Eden, Stephanie thought, shivering with delicious anticipation as Matteo removed her clothing and let his fingers drift over her bare skin, it surely resembled heaven close enough that she didn't care if she never knew the real thing.

He came to her quietly. Buried himself inside her in one smooth glide of hot, potent masculinity. Once there, he rested on his forearms and looked down at her, his eyes dark and intent.

He moved once, a deep, urgent thrust. "Do you know why I left you before?" he asked thickly. Another thrust, quick and imperative. "*Do* you, Stephanie?"

Yes," she said, the word escaping on a breathless sigh. "I wanted more than you could give me."

"Wrong, *tesoro.*" A third peremptory incursion, so

penetrating this time that she felt its effect reverberate clear throughout her body, a lovely resounding echo of leashed passion. "Because I was afraid of the feelings you aroused in me—the emotions I wasn't able to control."

She dug her fingers into his shoulders, lifted her hips to meet his. "You weren't ready, Matteo."

"I'm ready now," he ground out, and she saw the sweat, cast in shades of blood from the dying sunset, gleaming on his forehead.

She wrapped her legs around his waist, any fear of discovery by strangers long forgotten. Let them line up and sell tickets, if it pleased them! Her world had narrowed to exclude anyone but Matteo. He *was* her world, and she wanted all of him, the hot spill of his seed secreted in her body, the fevered heat of his kiss branding her his forever.

Whatever was wrong with their past, whatever setbacks they might face tomorrow, this moment between her and him was as right, as honest, and as perfect as anything ever could be, and she ached desperately for a permanent keepsake, something to immortalize the experience.

God help her, she wanted his baby. Again! And when his body fused with hers in an explosive culmination of passion, she experienced a brief but piercing sense of loss that, as always, he'd taken the precaution of using a condom.

Of course, sanity returned faster than her hectic breathing grew calm. Quickly enough for her to be grateful that he, at least, had shown responsible foresight. But not, alas, soon enough to stem words which wouldn't be held back any longer.

"I love you, Matteo," she whispered, trembling all over from the pure emotional catharsis of finally putting into words that which had lain repressed in her heart for such a long, long time. "I love you so much!"

He lifted his head and gazed down at her, his dark eyes troubled. "You're shivering, Stephanie."

"Not really," she said, even though her teeth rattled.

"But yes!" He sprang to his feet and reached for her clothing, spread haphazardly on the sand. "What a selfish brute I am! Here, *cara*, let me help you dress."

All at once chilled in a way that owed nothing to the outside temperature, she stood passively as he pulled her blouse over her shoulders. "Did you hear what I said, Matteo?"

"I heard." He knelt to pull her underpants up her legs. Lifted her feet, one at a time, to slip on her sandals.

Staring at the broad, tanned expanse of his shoulders, at the luxurious thickness of his dark, shining hair, she asked hollowly, "Is that all you have to say?"

"You took me by surprise, that is all." Suddenly sounding inscrutably foreign, he shook the sand from her skirt and passed it to her, then busied himself with his own clothing.

Instinct told her not to pursue the matter further, but hurt pride had her wailing, "You'd rather I kept quiet, don't you?"

"Of course not," he said. "What man does not wish to hear such words from his woman?"

"This man, apparently!"

"Not so, Stephanie. I just don't believe you mean them."

"How can you doubt it?" she cried.

"Because you speak out of fear. When you trust me enough to say *I love you* unhindered by reservation, you may be sure I'll welcome hearing it." He sighed heavily, as though striving for patience. "This isn't the same as before, Stephanie. I'm not going to hurt you this time."

His insight and candor devastated her. If he'd driven a

stake through her heart, he could not have wounded her more deeply. "What if I hurt you?" she whispered.

"You won't. You don't have it in you to inflict pain."

Oh, dear God!

Tell him everything now! her shattered conscience urged.

She could not. *Let me have these few precious days first,* she begged, *before the light in his eyes grows dark with anger, and his voice turns cold and distant, and he no longer cares whether or not I love him, because all he feels for me is disgust and hatred!*

CHAPTER TEN

STEPHANIE'S self-possession, already badly cracked by his too-astute assessment of her inner turmoil, fell apart completely when she laid eyes on what Matteo off-handedly referred to as "the family *casa*."

She'd anticipated something small and pretty, not unlike his cottage on Ischia, with bougainvilleas climbing up pale, ice-cream colored walls, and a paved path leading through the garden. She'd imagined his mother dressed in severe black as befit an Italian widow well into her sixties, and his grandmother, positively ancient, also wearing black. She'd envisioned the pair of them hovering at the front door, nervously waiting to welcome home the beloved only son, and the woman threatening to replace them in his affections.

Instead, the car turned in between stone-pillared gates, and proceeded up a long driveway lined with ancient cypresses, at the end of which the residence sat majestically among a vast spread of immaculately tended gardens. As it swam into view between the trees, like a vision from an era of classic elegance long past, Stephanie's jaw dropped. To refer to such a gem as a mere "house" was such a massive understatement as to be absurd. The villa's magnificent facade alone was enough to elevate it to baronial stature.

"You don't live here!" she exclaimed, utter shock rendering her words less a question than an absolute statement of fact.

He cast her a lazy, amused glance. "Why not?"

"Well…because….!" She floundered to find an answer, something that wouldn't come out sounding insultingly condescending. "Because it's too big for two old women to live in alone."

Oh, for crying out loud! If that tactless response was the best she could come up with on short notice, she'd be better off keeping her mouth shut altogether.

But far from taking offense, he grinned and said, "They entertain a lot. For *two old women*, they're quite a lively pair."

"But, Matteo…!" Unable to draw her gaze away, she continued to stare in stunned wonder at the perfect symmetry and grace of the building before her. Supported by four Greek columns, the central section stood two floors high, with single-storied wings extending from each side. Although the windows and front door of the main part were rectangular, those running the width of the wings rose in tall, elegant arches. "This is the most beautiful place I've ever seen."

"And much too grand for a lowly quarry worker?"

"I didn't say that," she insisted defensively, but knew her fiery blush put the lie to her words. "It's just that…well, you live in a gardener's cottage, on Corinna's property, when you could obviously afford…!" She clapped a hand to her mouth, as awareness dawned.

"The much more impressive villa next door, which I inherited from my grandfather and which is currently occupied by my very dear old friends from Canada, and their dysfunctional family members?" he supplied. "The idea appears to dismay you, Stephanie. Why is that?"

"I'm not dismayed," she said haltingly. "It's just that you've never mentioned you're…." She stumbled into silence, shying way from the only word that sprang to mind.

"Rich?" He said it for her.

Once again, she scrambled to compose a reply. But this

was one time when bald truth was the only option. "Well...since you put it that way, yes!"

He brought the car to a stop in the forecourt and cocked another amused glance her way. "Should I have?" he asked silkily. "Does it matter whether I'm rich or poor?"

She was spared having to come up with an answer to that by the appearance of a tall, dignified manservant who hurried from the villa to open the driver's side door. "Welcome home, *Signor* Matteo," he said, then came around to Stephanie's side. *"Buona sera, Signora."*

"Buona sera," she managed, her mind spinning madly.

"Welcome to the *Villa Valenti.*"

"Thank you." Still dazed, she clutched his hand gratefully as he helped her alight.

"Grazie, Emanuel." Matteo tossed the car keys to him and took her arm. "My mother and grandmother are in the evening salon, are they?"

"Sì, Signor." The man's face broke into a smile. "And the champagne is chilling."

"Eccellente!" Matteo shepherded Stephanie toward the house. "Brace yourself, *tesoro!* It's time to meet the dragon ladies." He put his mouth close to her ear, and in a low voice added, "One more thing: try not to stare at my grandmother's mustache or she'll put the evil eye on you. Oh, yes, and my mother has two fingers missing on her right hand—an accident when she was helping out in the marble quarry as a child. It's best that you be forewarned, to avoid any awkwardness, *sì?*"

Dragon ladies? Mustache? Evil eye and missing fingers?

Good grief, what next?

Stephanie hung back, desperately needing a few minutes to compose herself. Too much was happening, much too fast. She wasn't prepared for any of this. But Matteo was in no mood to delay, and practically galloped her through the carved front door and into a grand entrance foyer.

Passing from there through a wide, softly lit central hall, she gathered a fleeting impression of high painted ceilings, marble floors, gilt framed portraits and masses of fresh-cut flowers arranged in huge jardinieres. Then, before she could catch her breath, let alone any semblance of poise, he was flinging open a door at the rear of the house, and thrusting her willy-nilly into a tastefully appointed sitting room decorated in shades of aquamarine with white accents.

Stephanie's eye was drawn inexorably to the two women sitting opposite each other on sumptuously upholstered couches near the window. Immediately, the so-called dragon ladies rose in unison and came forward, uttering melodic cries of pleasure.

The taller, younger one, obviously Matteo's mother, was a dark-haired, strikingly handsome woman with a wide smile and an air of unshakable serenity. Her dress, a superbly cut, simple cream silk, fell in graceful folds to mid-calf. Her heeled shoes were the same rich shade as the garnet studs in her ears and the ornate dinner ring on her right hand.

His grandmother's thick white hair was swept up in an elegant twist and held in place with a silver clasp. She wore an ankle length crepe silk skirt in deep blue, with a matching top, a string of jet beads and pendant earrings, and was quite the most fashion-conscious octagenarian Stephanie ever expected to meet.

Making no bones about it, she examined Stephanie from head to toe. All at once dismally conscious of the grains of sand in her hair, the damp aftermath of love-making and—dear heaven, the scent of passion, of sex!—clinging to her skin, Stephanie almost cringed under that penetrating inspection.

"Finalmente, you are here!" Matteo's mother exclaimed, reaching up to kiss him, then stepping aside to allow his grandmother to fold him in a long, exuberant hug.

He accepted it all with good grace before disentangling himself and, placing his arm around Stephanie's waist, drew her into their tight little circle of affection. *"Madre, Nonna, posso presentami* Stephanie Leyland-Owen? Stephanie, this is my mother, *Signora* De Luca, and my grandmother, *Signora* Berlusconi."

His mother raised her hands—both with a full complement of fingers flawlessly manicured, Stephanie noticed—framed Stephanie's face, and kissed her on each cheek. "We are very delighted to welcome you to our home," she cooed warmly, in accented but perfect English. "Are we not, *Madre?"*

"Sì," the spritely grandmother agreed, kissing Stephanie also. Though slightly wrinkled with age and from many summers of hot Tuscan sunshine, her face bore not a trace of a mustache, and although her black eyes snapped with lively interest, they showed no inclination to cast evil on anyone. If anything, the lines fanning from their corners indicated she'd done a lot of laughing in her time. "And you will call me *Nonna. Signora* Berlusconi is a full mouth, is it not?"

"You mean, a mouthful, *Nonna,"* Matteo said, playing the jovial innocent to the hilt. "You have to be careful what you say to Stephanie. She might misunderstand and jump to all the wrong conclusions."

I will throttle him, the first chance I get! Stephanie promised herself, shooting him a malignant glare.

He answered with a disarming grin, and grasped the foil-covered neck of a bottle of wine cooling in the silver ice bucket on a nearby library table. "Champagne, everyone?"

"But of course!" Ushering her mother and guest to the couches, *Signora* De Luca sat down next to Stephanie. "We must make the most of this evening to get to know one another, *cara*," she confided. "I fear it's the only time we'll have you to ourselves. Others in our family are anxious to meet you and will be arriving tomorrow."

Matteo scowled. "Not all the cousins, I hope!" he said, serving the wine in wafer thin champagne flutes delicately etched with what Stephanie suspected was the family coat of arms. "I want to show Stephanie around, not show her off."

"You will have time," his mother promised. "We have arranged a small dinner party for tomorrow night, and a simple luncheon for Sunday, that is all. I will entertain the rest of the family while you take Stephanie on a tour of our countryside."

But words like "small" and "simple" took on quite a different meaning in that opulently elegant world, Stephanie soon realized. When she was shown to her bedroom in the east wing, to freshen up before dinner, it turned out to be a suite with an adjoining sitting room, and a private bathroom so luxurious that she'd have been happy to spend the entire evening soaking in the deep, marble tub, instead of settling for a quick scrub in the glass-enclosed shower stall. The furnishings throughout, from the delicate four-poster bed hung with silk, to the carved writing desk and charming little slipper chair, were fit for a princess.

Dinner for four involved six courses, prepared by the resident cook and presented by the butler Emmanuel. It meant fine Tuscan wines served in cut crystal stemware, heavy sterling silver, monogrammed hand-stitched linens, and gorgeous antique china rimmed in royal blue and bearing the family crest in twenty-four carat gold. It meant Matteo put on a dark suit with a starched white shirt and silk tie, and his mother and grandmother changed into dinner dresses and wore diamonds.

Thank heavens he'd forewarned her to bring something dressy for the evenings, Stephanie thought, unobtrusively tugging her ivory beaded top over the waist of her long black taffeta skirt. He'd already set her at enough of a disadvantage with his high jinks. She'd never have forgiven him if he'd let her walk any more unprepared into his home than he already had.

And yet, she was forced to admit later, when the evening was over and she was at last free to soak up to her neck in scented water in her wonderful marble tub, wasn't it just as much her fault that he'd managed to bamboozle her so thoroughly? That she'd been hoodwinked at nineteen was, perhaps excusable. But to be so easily duped at twenty-nine?

Hardly! The evidence that he was much more than she'd supposed he was had been there from the outset, if only she'd cared to recognize it.

The way he conducted himself—his self-possession and sophistication, not to mention his membership in an obviously exclusive supper club on Ischia, and his relationship with Corinna who, by her own admission, regarded him not only as a friend of long-standing, but also as a social equal—all pointed to a man of privileged upbringing. Reduced to its most crass level, Matteo De Luca's claim to gentility far exceeded anything Stephanie's father and brother aspired to, and rendered *her* little more than a superficial fool.

Groaning, she slid down in the tub until she was fully submerged. She had never been so mortified in her life. And the worst was yet to come because she still had to tell him about Simon. How much sympathetic understanding had she a right to expect, given her own lack of sensitivity?

It was a question which hounded her mercilessly throughout Friday and most of Saturday. It spoiled the pleasure she'd have taken in learning the history of the villa, which had been designed by the famous sixteenth century architect Andrea Palladio. She was barely able to drum up a word of appreciation for the Veronese frescoes decorating the interior of the residence, or the marble statuary scattered throughout the formal gardens.

By the time she was shown the beautiful little private chapel behind the main house, "where our *matrimonios* take place, and our *bambinos* are baptized," *Nonna* informed her with a sly wink, Stephanie was hard-pressed to contain her wretchedness. There were, she learned, many churches worldwide, endowed with altars and statues created from marble hewn from De Luca and Berlusconi quarries in Carrara. But none, she was sure, were as exquisitely depicted as the altar and touchingly serene figure of the Virgin Mary holding the infant Jesus, that graced the Villa Valenti's *cappella.*

How differently might her and Matteo's lives have played out, had they both been more open with each other from the beginning; if she'd told him she was pregnant and he'd admitted that he cared! Simon might then have been born into this close-knit, loving family, instead of one torn apart by silly pretension.

There would have been no running away, no disastrous marriage to Charles, no deception, no shame. Even at nineteen, and after years of being the dutiful, obedient daughter, with Matteo by her side she'd have found the strength to stand up to her overbearing father. Been able to dismiss Victor's mocking scorn for what it truly was: totally irrelevant to anything of importance in her life.

She could have provided stauncher support for her long-suffering mother. Caused her grandparents less worry. Because they had always known she harbored a deep unhappiness. They just hadn't known why.

Instead, she had caved in to pressure, and now faced the daunting task of admitting openly how much she had stolen from Matteo, his family, and from Simon himself.

They had missed his babyhood—his first smile, his first tooth, his first step. Missed his first stage appearance, as a toadstool in his preschool's Easter play. Missed his first piano recital, when he'd been so delighted with the applause following his performance that he'd played *Jingle Bells* three more times before his teacher had persuaded him enough was enough.

They hadn't been there when he'd scored his first soccer goal, or shot his first basketball three-pointer. They hadn't shared the magic of his first Christmas. They had no idea he hated peanut butter and loved calamari. Or that she'd given him the middle name of Matthew in honor of his biological father.

They knew nothing about him, nor he about them, and it was all her fault.

"You look sad, *cara*," Matteo's mother remarked, cornering her during the cocktail hour on Saturday evening. She inclined her head to the mob of relatives chattering noisily on the terrace. "We are too much to take in all at once, is that it?"

They were, but not in the way *Signora* De Luca supposed. It might have helped if they'd been so immersed in visiting one another that they had no time for the foreigner in their midst! But they'd welcomed her without a moment's hesitation, and their warm generosity of spirit did nothing to soothe the raw hurt festering inside her. Rather, such undeserved acceptance added to Stephanie's already onerous burden of guilt.

Somehow she managed to control her quivering chin. This woman's gentle compassion was hard to take, when it might well turn to disgust before the weekend was out. "I was thinking about my son," she said.

"Simon, isn't it? Matteo speaks very fondly of him. You miss your little boy?"

"Oh, *Signora* De Luca!" Stephanie fought the lump in her throat and blinked rapidly. "I wish that's all there was to it."

"You worry that, if you pursue a relationship with my son, he might not accept yours?" Matteo's mother touched her arm kindly. "Don't concern yourself about that, Stephanie. Matteo will be a very good father to your boy, and we will take him to our hearts, just as we've taken you."

"I'm afraid," she quavered, perilously close to breaking down, "you might not feel the same if you knew...."

"Knew what, *cara mia?*"

"About Simon—about who his real father is!" Stephanie cried, the whole guilty weight of her secret becoming more than she could bear a second longer.

Matteo's mother glanced out to the terrace, seemed satisfied that her guests were managing very well without her, and quickly led Stephanie from the salon and down the hall to the library. Once there, she pressed her into a chair, poured her an inch of brandy from the decanter on the desk, and waited until she'd downed it, before saying, "Then Simon is not your late husband's son?"

Oozing shame from every pore, Stephanie cast down her eyes and shook her head. "No."

"And Matteo does not know this?"

"No."

"Why not?"

Her voice sank until it was barely audible. "Because I'm afraid to tell him...who is."

The following silence swelled until she thought she would suffocate on it. It stretched and swirled around her, thick and heavy, robbing her of the ability to breathe. The blood pounded in her head. Her heart bounced erratically behind her ribs. Perspiration prickled down her spine and left her hands damp.

At last, *Signora* De Luca asked, "Is it Matteo, Stephanie?"

A sob burst from her lips—a great, ugly wrenching sound that tore her apart. She couldn't speak. She didn't need to. Matteo's mother knew, without her having to say a word.

"Per carita!" she exclaimed in soft wonder. "After all these years of praying for just such a gift, God has given me a grandson."

She walked to the window. Stared out at the moon rising above the cypresses. At the hills etched clear against the night sky. At length she said, "Are you ever going to share this with Matteo?"

"Yes. I planned to tell him this weekend. But I didn't know until we arrived that we were staying here. I didn't know how much more difficult it would make it, to tell him such a thing once I'd met his family." Stephanie drew in a painful breath. "You've been so kind, so welcoming, and I'm sure, now that you know the terrible lie I've perpetrated, that you wish you'd never met me."

Signora De Luca considered the matter for several long, tense moments before replying, "On the contrary, you are my grandson's mother, Stephanie, and for that reason alone will always be welcome in my home. *Non piangere, cara.* I can't speak for Matteo—how he will take this news, what it will do to your relationship—but I can promise you he will not walk away from his son. And lest you continue punishing yourself so harshly for your mistake, let me remind you that you did not conceive this child alone. Whatever the reason you didn't feel able to tell Matteo sooner, it in no way changes the fact that he must bear half the responsibility for the situation now facing the two of you.''

Shockingly, there came a knock at the door just then. Sure it must be Matteo and that the hour of reckoning was at hand, Stephanie leaped out of the chair in a panic. But it was *Nonna* who came into the room.

"So this is where you have hidden yourselves,'' she said, her wise old gaze swinging from her daughter's face to Stephanie's, and missing nothing. ''There is trouble, *sì?*''

"*Sì,*'' *Signora* De Luca replied, and waited until her mother had closed the door before stating the facts without preface or mitigation. ''Matteo is the father of Stephanie's son.''

"I'm not surprised,'' *Nonna* replied calmly. ''They met many years ago and one has only to see how they look at one another to know that a great passion burns between them, one much too fierce to have sprung up in the short time that Stephanie has been in *Italia.*''

"The point is, *Madre mia,* Matteo has no idea that the child is his.''

Nonna shrugged. ''Men are always the last to see what is staring them in the face. I was five months along before your father knew I carried you in my belly. More significant at this moment is that Matteo is now looking for Stephanie and will probably discover her here very soon. It would best, *la mia figlia,* that we leave before he arrives. This is not a business to be sorted out in front of others.''

She approached Stephanie and pressed a warm kiss to her cheeks. "*Non piangere, bambina!* We are here if you need us.''

"*Sì,*'' Matteo's mother hastened to add. ''Whatever the outcome, you may count on our support, Stephanie.''

A moment later, she found herself alone, but the respite

lasted only a short while. As predicted, Matteo showed up soon after and one look at her face was all it took for him to recognize that something was sadly amiss.

"You've been crying," he said, coming to where she stood and wrapping her in his arms. "What is it, *cara?* What's happened?"

Just for a second, she allowed herself to lean into his strength. To savor the feel of his arms around her, the beat of his heart next to hers, the scent of him.

He smelled like no other man she'd ever met—of masculine cologne, and fine cotton shirts dried in the sweet, clean air of Tuscany and stored with a sachet of dried herbs tucked between them, to keep them fresh for when he next came home and wore them. For the rest of her life, the sharp scent of rosemary would bring him alive in her memory.

He stepped back and gazed at her in consternation. *"Per favore, non piangere,* sweetheart!" he begged.

Non piangere—don't cry! The words were carved forever in her heart, and to her dying day she'd never forget them. She'd heard them from his mother, his grandmother, and most of all, from him—uttered with concern, with compassion, with kindness, with love. And soon, he wouldn't care if she cried for the rest of her life.

"I'm trying not to!" she hiccuped, her reply so riddled with sobs as to be barely distinguishable.

He frowned and caught her chin with his thumb, forcing her face up to meet his. "I passed my mother and grandmother on the way here. Surely they're not the reason you're so upset?"

She scrubbed at the tears streaming down her face. *"No!* Your mother and grandmother are two of the finest people in the world and have shown me more kindness than I will ever deserve."

"Nonsense!" he said. "What kind of thing is that to say?"

She pulled away from him, knowing she could put matters off no longer, and drew in a long, shuddering breath. "Matteo, there is something I've been keeping from you."

"I know. I've known it all along." He turned suddenly pale under his tan. "Are you ill, *cara?* Is that it?"

"No. Sick, perhaps, but not in the way you suppose."

He grew very still and it seemed to her that a shutter came down over his face, shielding his emotions. "Then what are you trying to say, Stephanie?"

"I have something to confess and I'm afraid, once you hear, that you'll never look at me the same way again."

"Perhaps you should let me be the judge of that."

"You might want to sit down."

"I do not wish to sit down. I wish you to state what is on your mind, and I wish you to do so *now.*"

She swallowed. Suddenly he was very much the aristocratic Italian, very proud, very distant. His eyes were cool, his expression remote. "Is there someone else?" he inquired coldly.

"No!" she cried, appalled that he'd even think such a thing. "I love *you* and only you!"

He spread out his hands, palms upturned. "Then whatever it is can't be so bad."

No? The pent-up angst gnawing holes in her stomach made a mockery of his confidence. Struggling to couch her news in such a way that it would sound *good* was hopeless.

At her wit's end, and knowing that time had finally run out on her, she condensed all the speeches she'd rehearsed into one disastrously bald statement. "Simon isn't Charles's son, Matteo. He's yours," she said.

CHAPTER ELEVEN

She had guts, he'd grant her that much. Guts and gall! Sitting at his left hand at dinner, she projected an air of superb poise, accepting as if it were her due the effusive compliments showered on her by his unsuspecting family.

Only he, who knew her well—though not, it appeared, nearly as well as he'd believed—saw through her act and recognized the cool blue light in her eyes for what it really was: a proud shield behind which she hid her mental disarray.

He's not Charles's son...he's yours....

Just so, had she tossed the news at him, then stood back and watched the fall-out.

Simon, of the blond hair and blue eyes, his son? Matteo had reeled at the idea. "Impossible!" he'd scoffed.

"If DNA proof is what it takes to convince you," she said, with a curious lack of emotion, "it can be arranged."

Who did she think she was, that she could play fast and loose like that with other people's lives?

But that side of his brain remaining detached from the unfolding scene had told him he didn't need laboratory proof. Stephanie wasn't lying. A bone-deep instinct that approached paranormal proportions told him she was speaking the truth, perhaps for the first time since he'd known her.

What made it so much worse, though, was that he'd actually wondered, back when she'd first arrived on Ischia and been so skittish every time she saw him, if he could possibly be her son's father. Something about the boy, the easy way he'd connected with the child, had struck a strangely unnerving chord.

And damn him—*damn her!*—he'd ignored it. Decided she was too scrupulously honest to pull off such a deception. Decided it was just wishful thinking on his part, and that he'd be better off concentrating his attention on *her,* the primary object of his affections, and forgetting about Simon until he'd reeled in Stephanie.

What point was there, after all, in disrupting the kid's life if he, Matteo, was not destined to be a vital part of it? Time enough to cement a bond with the boy when he knew the mother was his for the asking.

"Un brindisi!" From the other end of the table, his slightly inebriated second cousin, Jacomo, struck his wineglass with his fork, bringing all eyes on him. "To Matteo and his lovely *Canadesa* Stephanie! Welcome to our family, *Signora!"*

"Grazie," she murmured, behaving exactly as a well brought-up Leyland should. Masking her misery behind a thin, impenetrable reserve, and responding with the subdued courtesy of the perfect guest not about to take more for granted than was willingly offered.

But Matteo saw how tightly she gripped the stem of her wineglass. Saw how she fought to control the agitated rise and fall of her breasts beneath the filmy dark blue fabric of her dress.

If his mother or grandmother noticed her distraction, they gave no sign. Instead, as Jacomo entertained everyone with snatches of song from *The Marriage of Figaro,* they showered her with warm, encouraging smiles. Nodded their approval. Did damn near everything but stand up and proclaim her their future daughter-in-law.

"You don't have to," she'd admitted in a trembling whisper, when he'd demanded of her how he should break news of his son to his immediate family. "I've already told them."

He'd sworn fluently and thrown a savage punch at the wall. "So I'm the last to know?"

Unable to look him in the eye, she'd cast her glance aside and nodded. "I didn't mean for it to come out like this, Matteo."

"I'm sure you didn't," he'd replied. "I'm sure, if you had things your way, you'd have gone to your grave without telling a soul."

She'd swung back to face him at that. "No! I had every intention of confessing to you before this weekend was over. I couldn't bear the guilt a moment longer."

"So you chose now to rid yourself of it, with the house full of relatives in a party mood? Why, Stephanie? Did you think their presence would force me to meekly accept this astounding revelation, and spare you the consequences of your actions?"

"Listen to me," she'd begged, trying to grab hold of his hands, a move he'd avoided with unbridled distaste. He wanted none of her—not the touch of her soft, smooth skin, not her lying mouth, not her piteous, tear-glazed eyes. "I didn't—"

"Save it!" he spat.

"But I have to explain, Matteo!"

"You most assuredly do, but at a time of my choosing, not yours. At this moment, my mother's household staff is waiting to serve a celebratory dinner destined to last well into the evening. We have fourteen visiting family members eager to sit down at our table, and unable to do so because etiquette demands they wait until the guest of honor chooses to join them—not, I suppose, that you ever expected any blood relative of mine to recognize the rules of socially acceptable behavior, let alone abide by them."

Ignoring his sarcasm, she cried, "I can't face them! Not with this hanging over us."

"Why ever not, *cara* Stephanie, *la mia bella bugiardo?* You've managed to conduct yourself with admirable aplomb this far, despite your professed burden of guilt. What's another hour or two, or ten? What's another day, or week?"

"Please, Matteo, don't force me to go through with this. Make my excuses, I'm begging you!"

"Not a chance in hell! You might not care one iota about embarrassing yourself, but I will not permit you to embarrass me or my family. So wipe the *falso* grief from your deceiving face and replace it with something more suited to the occasion."

"I won't!" she said brokenly. "I *can't!*"

He did touch her then, clamping his hand around the delicate skin of her upper arm and marching her to the door. "You can, and you will."

She could, and she had! The animated talk, the level of laughter as his cousins reminisced about childhood exploits and misdemeanors, Jacomo's irrepressible urge to serenade the party growing stronger with each glass of wine he consumed, told Matteo clearly enough that they all remained unaware of the steely tension stretching between him and her.

The conviviality scraped his nerves raw. He wanted to slam the flat of his hand on the surface of the long polished table, hard enough to rattle the sterling silver and send the heavy crystal skidding. Wanted to bellow his pain and outrage for the whole world to hear.

Cloaking his churning emotions, he leaned back, toyed with his glass, laughed in all the right places, and generally projected the air of a relaxed host enjoying the good company of his nearest and dearest. Everyone was too busy having a good time to notice that he contributed little to the conversation, or that Stephanie's head drooped like a fading flower on the delicate stem of her neck. None but he saw the lone tear drizzle down her cheek, to be swallowed up by her napkin as she made a pretense of dabbing the corner of her mouth.

That she ate nothing of the food placed before her was something only Emanuel realized. The ultimate inscrutable *maggiordomo,* he betrayed not a vestige of surprise and merely whisked away her untouched plate, and replaced it with another.

Matteo wished he could take pleasure in what he observed of her misery. He wished knowing that she'd brought it on herself gave him satisfaction. He wished he could hate her.

Instead, her fragile inner core undid him. He had every right to despise her for all she'd denied him and their son. But damn her, he couldn't ignore the crushed vulnerability in her eyes, the sad and trembling curve of her mouth.

And it infuriated him.

The chance to escape didn't arise until everyone moved from the dining hall to the evening salon, for espresso and *grappa.* In the ensuing hullabaloo, Stephanie managed to slip through the door to the east wing without anyone noticing.

The enormous strain of preserving a front before a roomful of well-intentioned strangers had taken a fearsome toll. Physically and emotionally drained, she sagged against the wall and listened as the buzz of voices, bursts of laughter, and occasional snatches of operatic aria faded to a distant murmur.

She envied Matteo his large, close-knit family, so different from her own, but tonight they exhausted her. Nothing they offered in the way of diversion could take her mind off the disastrous events before dinner, and not all their collective warmth was enough to counteract the pervading chill of Matteo's icy displeasure.

Dejectedly, she leaned against the window and gazed out on a night freckled with stars; a night so beautiful that it hurt to look at it. One so haunted with pain and useless regret that she wished she could wipe the memory of it clean from her mind, and knew she'd never be able to.

At length, she marshaled her flagging energy, and stumbled down the long hall to her suite of rooms. Of course, he'd be furious that she'd deserted the party. But any more furious than he already was? She doubted that was possible. And regardless, she was at the end of her social rope.

Matteo's outrage and her own beleaguered attempt not to disgrace herself in front of his family had, of necessity, taken precedence thus far into the evening. But the other half of the equation had lurked in the background long enough and was no longer content to take second billing.

How could she minimize the damage already inflicted on her relationship with Matteo? And more important, how did she permit the truth of Simon's paternity to emerge without shattering the child's trust?

"Your dead husband and I aren't interchangeable parts," Matteo had raged, when she'd dared suggest he could at long last assume his rightful place in his son's life.

"But if I explain—"

"What? That you wilfully misled him, and knowingly kept his real father from him all these years? How does your warped little mind justify having done that, Stephanie?"

Plainly put, there *was* no justification. *Nothing* excused denying a boy his father, or a father his child. Whatever had made her think differently?

Defeated before she'd even begun to resolve the crisis

her life had become, she pushed open the door to her suite. It swung silently inward to reveal the moon shining its light through the tall Palladian windows and turning to dull silver everything it touched.

This, she thought, surveying the scene through a mist of tears, was Simon's true inheritance. Not the material wealth represented by the elegant antique furnishings, but the legacy of timeless security inherent in the very atmosphere of the place. She had robbed him of that, of the acceptance of this loving family, and subjected him instead to life with a single mother whose need to provide well for him had necessitated placing him in the care of strangers.

How could she expect him to believe she'd thought she was acting in his best interests?

Wretchedly, she stooped to take off her high-heeled satin pumps and made her way barefoot over the smooth marble floor to the bedroom. The *domestica* had turned back the covers on the four-poster, and left a lamp burning on the mirrored dressing table, and a thermos of ice water on the nightstand.

The plump pillows and cool white sheets offered temporary solace from all that beset her, and Stephanie, so bone weary she could barely stand, didn't even try to resist the escape they promised. Now was not the time to figure out how she was going to cope with the crucial situation facing her. Not with exhaustion sapping her of the ability to think clearly.

Someone once said that the darkest hour lay just before dawn, and who was she to argue the point? Maybe things wouldn't look quite so black in the morning. Perhaps in sleep the answers she so desperately sought would come to her.

She stripped off her dress and hung it in the armoire, then removed her jewelry, and took a fresh nightgown from the tall chest of drawers. The sheer ordinariness of such rituals bolstered her spirits a little by reminding her that, no matter how bad things might seem at this very moment, life *did* go on. This day *would* pass.

But respite was not to be so easily come by, after all. Fifteen minutes later, when she emerged from the bathroom, she found Matteo waiting. Eyes glittering in the dim light, he advanced toward her, and he didn't need to put into words the fact that he was livid with rage. It oozed from every pore. Was printed in cold fury on his face, in the lethal clenching and releasing of his fists.

She'd always known him to be a man of great passion but she'd never thought to see it like this, corrupted by anger to an ugliness that left her quaking. She'd never thought she could be so afraid of him. But at that moment, fear rose up her throat and filled her mouth with metallic urgency.

Panic stricken, she darted for the door, frantic to escape. But he moved swiftly to block her exit, and instead of finding freedom, she blundered into the solid wall of his chest.

He held her to him, not with love but with the steely force of prison bars. To pit her strength against his was pointless. He could have lifted her clean off the floor without effort. Could have snapped her neck with one hand.

And at that moment, he looked capable of both.

Uttering a pitiful squeak of protest, she said, "Let me go!"

"Not," he said grimly, manacling her wrists in his long, strong fingers, "until I'm done with you. And that, my very dear Stephanie, will not be any time soon."

She tried to pry herself free, a move which achieved precisely nothing but a tightening of his punishing hold. "Do not make me hurt you, Stephanie," he warned, with soft and deadly menace.

"You already are," she retorted. "Your mother would be appalled if she knew you were here, terrorizing me like this. Your grandmother would be ashamed. As for what your son would think, if he could see you manhandling me…!"

She'd grabbed the accusations out of thin air, a last-ditch attempt to protect herself that carried with it very little hope of success. Amazingly, though, they stopped him as forcefully as if he'd been hit with a sledgehammer.

He released her so suddenly, she almost collapsed at his feet. Turned his head away, as if he couldn't face her. Inhaled long, unsteady, hissing breaths which left his shirt front trembling. "Is this what I've allowed you to reduce me to?" he muttered. "A mindless thug who turns to brute violence to resolve his troubles?"

"I'm very sorry, Matteo," she whispered. "I know how much I've hurt you."

At that, he turned his gaze on her again, and she flinched at the emptiness she saw in his eyes. "Do you?"

"Yes," she said. "Because I'm hurting, too. You can't begin to know the terrible pain I've endured in keeping such a secret from you."

His lashes swept down in slow disbelief. "You have one hell of a nerve, trying to solicit my sympathy for *your* pain, when you've singlehandedly rendered me incapable of rational thought or judgment."

She flung out her hands in mute appeal. "If it means anything at all, I've wished so many times that I'd done things differently. That I'd had the courage to tell you I was pregnant."

"Why didn't you?" he inquired cuttingly. "And don't bother making excuses about my having left your country. If you'd really wanted to contact me, all you ever had to do was ask your grandparents where I could be reached."

She met his glance head-on. "If I had done that, would

you have believed you were my baby's father? It's not as if we hadn't taken precautions. You were very confident that I was well protected from the risk of pregnancy."

"As confident as you were that I wasn't proper father material for a Leyland?"

"That thought never entered my head!"

"Of course it did, Stephanie!" he scoffed. "That's why you didn't bother to give me the benefit of the doubt. Instead, you ran off and found yourself a man better suited to the role, and married him so fast that you hardly had time to learn his name before you took it as your own, and passed off my child as his."

"I had to!" she cried. "But not for the reason you think. If my father had known my baby was illegitimate, he'd never have accepted him. I lied, but never because I was ashamed of you, Matteo. It was only ever to protect Simon."

"You lied because you're a coward. Because you wanted an easy way out," he said flatly. "What a joke, to think I was ever taken in by your wide-eyed innocence, your guileless protestations about the sanctity of family!"

Feeling she had nothing left to lose, she told him the rest. "I am even worse than you think. Although I intended to tell you about Simon before I left Italy, I wouldn't have done it yet if Corinna hadn't forced my hand."

"Corinna knows about this, too?" he flared. "*Dio*, is there no end to your betrayal, that you could parade such news before everyone but me?"

"She guessed the truth for herself. But it was always my dream that Simon would eventually know you're his father, Matteo."

"Your dream, perhaps. But you did nothing to make it a reality until Corinna left you no choice, and for that I must thank her. It is because of *her,* not *you,* that I'm now in a position to exercise my rights as a father."

The accusation fell from those same lips that had kissed her with love, with tenderness, with passion. But there was nothing of those in his tone, or his look, or his manner now. He was angry and cold; bent on vengeance and punishment. And she was afraid of him.

She sank onto the dressing table bench and twisted her fingers in her lap, beside herself with anguish. "How do I convince you how much I regret the lies I've told?"

His laugh scraped over her, harsh and unamused. "Don't ask me! You've lied so often in the last few weeks that I'm not sure you understand the meaning of truth. You can't open your mouth without perverting the facts."

"That's unfair, Matteo! Apart from not telling you about Simon, I've never lied to you."

"Really? Aren't you the one who told me, just yesterday, that this weekend was to be about just you and me?"

"Yes. And I meant every word!"

"But it's never been about just you and me, Stephanie. There's always been a third party known only to you, yet one about whom I had every right to be made aware. You don't call that wilful misrepresentation?"

How could she deny it? "When you put it that way, yes. But I'm not the only one at fault. You deceived me, too, letting me think you were someone different from what you really are."

"And you think that equals the score? That it makes what you've done less despicable?"

She couldn't look at him. She knew there was no comparison, that her sin was greater by far. She'd been wrong from the outset not to tell him about Simon. The only right thing she'd ever done where Matteo was concerned, was listen to her heart. It had never once let her down.

"Not by a long shot," she said. "But one thing I will

swear to, on my son's life, is that I love you. I have always loved you. And nothing is ever going to change that.''

''Nothing?'' he said, with such soft threat that goose bumps broke out over her skin. ''Not even if I tell you that it's *my* turn now, to have Simon live with me? You've had him for the first ten years, after all, so it would seem to be a fair division of time, and something to which I'm fully entitled, since, in another ten years, he'll be past the age when he needs either one of us to provide him with a roof over his head.''

''You wouldn't do that!'' she said, almost fainting with fear. ''You wouldn't make him choose between us.''

''Are you so sure?''

''Yes,'' she said, refusing to give in to the terror marauding her body and turning it into a mass of cowering flesh. ''You're angry now, Matteo, but you're not really a cruel man. You wouldn't try to take a boy away from his mother.''

He glared at her in silence, the light of battle in his eyes. And then, quite suddenly, it flickered and died. ''You're quite right,'' he agreed roughly. ''I wouldn't. Which means that you and I must arrive at some sort of compromise.''

''What sort of compromise?'' she asked, caught between relief and caution.

He paced the length of the room, and ended up at the window with his back to her. ''We can resolve this impasse very simply. We can marry, thereby eliminating any need to involve the courts in a custody battle, and at the same time give Simon the one thing he's never really known: *two* parents committed to his happiness and well-being. We will live here in *Italia*, far removed from the unpleasant influence of your father and elder brother. You robbed my grandfather of knowing my son, but you will not do the same to my mother or grandmother. How's that for a civilized solution, my dear *signora?*"

Civilized? Perhaps! But to be issued a proposal of marriage based on such cold, unforgiving terms, to have him call her "my dear *signora*" as if the words left poison on his tongue, flayed her to the bone.

"You hesitate, Stephanie," he remarked, swinging around to confront her again. "Did I forget something?"

"No," she said, "but answer me this. Would you still have asked me to marry you, if you hadn't learned Simon was your son?"

"Would you still be insisting you love me, if you hadn't seen for yourself that I'm not someone you need to keep hidden away from your society-conscious father?"

"Yes."

"Then I would have asked you to marry me. Just not for the same reason that I'm proposing it now, that's all. Before, it would have been because I trusted you enough to believe we could build a life together. It would have been a love match."

"And now?"

He shrugged. "Now, it's become a matter of convenience. It will be an arrangement, a contract drawn up by lawyers, including my legal adoption of my son, which I consider a necessity in order to protect both his rights and mine. Now, I will marry you for his sake, instead of my own."

"Love doesn't turn off just like that, Matteo!"

He smiled at her, a cruel curving of his beautiful mouth which conveyed not a scrap of warmth or feeling. "Just because I said the words doesn't mean I meant them."

Stunned by the calculated ruthlessness in his voice, she recoiled as if he'd slapped her. "Then why did you act as if you did? Why did you insist on reviving our relationship?''

''For the same reason that I started it, ten years ago. Because you are a worthy accessory to a man of my standing. Because I find you desirable. Even now, I am hot and hard for you. I see you sitting there, in your pretty little nightdress, and I imagine tearing it off you, and having you lying naked beneath me, with your legs entwined around me, and your soft cries driving me to madness.''

''Then what's holding you back?'' she cried recklessly, her voice brimming with tears. ''If that's all I can give you, why not take me?''

''Because I am disgusted by my weakness.'' He wheeled around and strode to the door. ''And because there are less degrading ways a man can satisfy his carnal needs.''

''Such as what? By going to another woman?''

He tossed her another smile over his shoulder. ''Use your imagination, Stephanie. God knows it's stood you in good stead in the past!''

He'd have left her on that note, if she'd let him. But she raced after him, nearly tripping as her nightgown wrapped its soft folds around her ankles, and although it took all her strength to do so, she caught his arm and wrenched him around to face her.

''You haven't changed at all,'' she told him, her own anger at last matching his. ''Underneath all your slick, sophisticated charm, you're still the same heartless brute you've always been. You've just learned to keep it better hidden, is all.''

''You are so right, Stephanie,'' he said softly. ''I am all that you accuse me of, and then some. Do you remember a time, not so very long ago, that I told you you had nothing to fear from me, that I was not asking for your firstborn?''

She froze, the moment, the context, rushing back to her in vivid detail. He had been trying to persuade her to go to dinner with him, the day she and Simon had run into him in *Ischia Porto,* and she had done her utmost to resist the invitation.

"I see that you remember only too clearly," he said, his unblinking, unforgiving gaze never once wavering from her face. "Well, I'm not asking now, Stephanie. I'm taking. One way or another, Simon *will* learn that I am his real father. He *will* learn as much as I can teach him about his Italian roots. And if you choose to come along for the ride, *va bene.* If you do not...." He raised his shoulders in an indolent shrug. "Then *arrivederci, cara mia.*"

CHAPTER TWELVE

THERE was no sleep for Stephanie, after that. She lay in the bed, reliving the exchange with Matteo, word by crushing word. And even though she repeatedly told herself his vitriolic attack had been prompted by anger, that he'd spoken in the heat of the moment, during the dark, fertile hours when nightmares crept in and chased out reason, his threat to steal Simon took root and flourished.

Such things *did* happen. The news was littered with stories of fathers kidnapping their own children; of mothers appearing on television and making tearful appeals to have their babies returned. Matteo De Luca was a fascinating mix of implacable will and burning passion. But bind the two together with a taste for vengeance and, if tonight's display was anything to go by, she'd be a fool to underestimate him. What he could not achieve by fair means, he'd achieve by foul.

And he had the means to do so. A private helicopter close by, ready for take-off at a moment's notice. Money. Influence. For her to think she could fight such a powerhouse on his own turf was absurd. If he were to spirit Simon away in what she now suspected were any number of places he owned, how effectively could she counter such actions in a country where she had no friends and didn't even speak the language?

She couldn't afford the risk of finding out, and by the time the sun rose, she knew what she had to do. Opportunity to put her plan into action was all she needed and, by happy circumstance, this fell into her lap when she joined the family in the breakfast room.

Several cousins had stayed overnight and were planning to spend the morning in Lucca—"at the antique market," they explained, bombarding her with the same unflagging enthusiasm they'd displayed at dinner. "It takes place on the third Sunday of every month, in the *Piazza Antelminelli* and *Piazza San Giusto*. Come with us, Stephanie. Learn something of our local traditions."

But she, casting a glance around the table and seeing no sign of Matteo, knew a surge of uneasiness. "Is Matteo going to be there as well?"

"No. He went riding earlier, and said he wouldn't be back until lunch," his mother told her, adding in an undertone as the general babble of conversation resumed, "He wanted to be alone for a while. You understand why, *sì?* He has much to think about."

In other words, he was avoiding her. Or plotting his next move. "And what time is lunch?"

"Two o'clock," *Signora* De Luca said. "We take our meals later on Sundays."

It was now nine o'clock. Five hours allowed ample time to carry out her plan. She'd be long gone before he even realized she was missing. "Then I'd love to see the market," she told the others. "How soon are you leaving?"

"As soon as you're ready," they said.

"I'm ready now." She pushed aside her coffee cup. "I seldom bother with breakfast."

Twenty minutes later, they'd all piled into three cars and were on their way. In order not to arouse suspicion, Stephanie carried only her purse. She'd send for the rest of her stuff once she and Simon were safely out of reach, and hope that *Signora* De Luca and *Nonna* would forgive her for leaving without thanking them. She would write to them later, and explain her reasons, and promise to bring Simon to meet them when the dust had settled.

They left the cars on the north edge of town, and proceeded on foot to the town center. It was, as Matteo had promised, a jewel of a place, with magnificent churches, palazzos, museums and gardens, and she'd have loved the chance to explore it at leisure. But she was a woman on a mission, and not about to waste a second of the time at her disposal.

Losing the cousins was easy. Once they'd entered the market area, they went their separate ways, arranging to meet later at an outdoor café in the *Piazza Antelminelli*. Pretending an interest in a gallery showing eighteenth century paintings, Stephanie waited until no one was looking, then slipped down a side street to where a sign outside a shop advertised cycles for rent. Ten minutes later, armed with a map, she was headed out of town on a quiet back road to the nearest airport, *Galileo Galilei*, in Pisa, some thirty kilometers away.

She'd covered about half the distance when she became aware of a car nosing up behind her. Steering as close to the edge of the road as possible, she waited for it to pass. Instead, it drew level.

It was a Ferrari. Low-slung and black. With Matteo behind the wheel.

He'd left her in a rage. Paced the night away in a fury. Met the new day full of pent-up frustration and doubt. And known he had to come to grips with his emotions before he saw her again.

Riding his favorite stallion in the hills behind the villa, with the cool, sweet air of a Tuscany morning blowing away his anger, he'd faced all the truth, instead of just part of it.

Yes, she'd kept knowledge of his son from him. But perhaps he'd driven her to such action by taking advantage of her innocence, then leaving her without a word.

And yes, since coming back into his life, she had continued the lie, but then he was no less guilty.

He had misled her. Taken secret enjoyment in the way she'd misunderstood his situation. Worse, he'd told her last night that he hadn't meant it when he said he loved her.

If she had played games, so had he. And in doing so, he'd lost sight of the bigger picture. Because, when all the raging and fury died to a whimper, what remained was that he loved her. He believed she loved him. And they had a son.

In the clear light of a new day, the enormity of such good fortune had struck home, and cutting short his ride, he returned to the villa, prepared to lay his heart bare before her. To cajole, instead of coerce. To coax instead of threaten.

He learned she'd gone to Lucca with his cousins, and followed, searching the antique market until he found them. Everyone but her. And one of his cousins mentioned seeing her enter the bike rental shop.

When Matteo inquired, the owner remembered the blond North American tourist. He'd supplied her with a bike for the day, and a map on which he'd marked the back road she should take. Because she wanted to see something of the countryside between Lucca and Pisa, she'd said.

But Matteo knew differently. She was running away again. With Simon. And it was all his fault. He jumped in the car, followed the road she'd taken and, within twenty minutes, caught sight of her pedaling furiously under the hot morning sun—a proud, willful, determined speck of humanity, with her blond hair flying out behind her, and her full skirt ballooning around like a parachute.

He started to smile. He couldn't help himself. Cruising into low gear, he idled the car alongside the bike. "Hey, *signora!''* he called through the open window. ''You're breaking the law, speeding like this. Pull over.''

''Get lost!'' she practically snarled. ''You want me to stop, you're going to have to run me off the road.''

Ahead, a wide green stretch speckled with wildflowers ran parallel to the road. ''That can be arranged,'' he said, and timed it perfectly, veering the Ferrari close enough to make her swerve into the long grass.

To his horror, though, instead of merely stopping, she went flying over the handlebars and landed in the grass. So hard, he thought she'd surely broken her neck. *He'd* broken her neck!

Dio! He slammed the car to a screeching standstill. Leaped out and raced to where she lay unmoving, face-down, with wildflowers springing up between the strands of her hair.

Anguished, he knelt beside her. Placed his hand on her ribs and felt his blood run cold when he discerned no perceptible sign that she was breathing. ''Stephanie!'' he whispered brokenly. ''*La mia innamorata,* what have I done?''

Her body gave a sudden lurch, her lungs heaved, her head popped up and she struggled to a sitting position. ''Tried to commit murder, if you ask me,'' she gasped, picking blades of grass out of her mouth.

So relieved he almost wept, he cradled her against his chest. ''I wanted to stop you, that's all. I never intended you harm.'' He eyed her anxiously. ''*Dove le fa male*— where does it hurt, *tesoro?*''

She flexed her ankles and shoulders. Rotated her wrists. Touched her midsection gingerly and winced. ''Here.''

''I must call an ambulance.''

He half rose, intending to go to his car phone, but she

grasped his arm. "I don't need an ambulance. I winded myself, that's all. I'll be fine in a minute."

"You don't look fine."

"I don't suppose I do," she said tartly. "You wouldn't, either, if you'd just done a face plant in a field, or spent the night walking the floor, worrying that the man you thought you knew might try to steal your child."

"I would never have done that."

"So you say now. But it was a different story last night."

"Last night, I was not myself. I spoke out of hurt pride and anger."

"No. You spoke out of conviction, Matteo." Her eyes grew stormy and her voice shook. "But so do I when I tell you that I will die before I let you take away my baby."

He snorted, thinking Simon might very well have done the same, had he heard his mother referring to him as a baby. "You will live—with me!—and spare us both any such tragedy."

"Another ultimatum?" She glared at him but this time, he saw, her eyes were bright with unshed tears. "Is my-way-or-the-highway how you usually conduct business?"

"*We* are not business, Stephanie," he said. "We are a man and woman who have fought the inevitable long enough, and it's high time we accepted that we were destined for one another from the start."

"Because of Simon?"

He cupped her face in his hands. "Because I love you and I believe that you love me. Because I can't imagine my life without you. And yes, because I want to take my rightful place as Simon's father. I want it all, Stephanie, just as I'm prepared to give all. That's the kind of man I am."

She turned her face and pressed her sweet mouth to his palm. "If only it were that easy."

"Love is never easy, *cara mia*," he said, his heart swelling in his chest at her simple gesture. "It is wild and complicated and greedy and unreasonable. It is what compelled me to drive us both to this madness today."

"Both!" she scoffed. "I'm not the one who ran you off the road!"

"Indeed not. You are the one who devised such a crazy plan to escape me." He nodded at the bike lying abandoned on the grass and was hard-pressed not to give in to another smile. "How far did you really think you'd get on that thing?"

"To the nearest airport, and from there to Ischia, to Simon. And from there home to Canada, with my son at my side."

"And if I told you that I wouldn't try to stop you? That if that's still what you want, you're free to go, and I'll even drive you to the airport in Pisa?"

She gave him another sour glare. "It didn't take you long to decide you could manage without us, did it?"

"That's not what I'm saying, Stephanie."

"Then what did you mean?"

"That I'll follow you to the ends of the earth, if that's what it takes to be near you."

"But your home is here."

"Yes. But if I must choose between here and wherever you are—"

"I'd never ask you to do that. *Italy* is your home, and I...I could learn to love living here."

"What about your life in Canada, your career?"

"My life would be with you. As for my career, it's served its purpose. Now what I'd most like is the luxury to be a full-time mother and wife." She sighed and leaned her head on his chest. "Am I asking too much, Matteo?"

"No," he said. "Not even a little bit."

"And can we really make it work?"

"*Sì*, if we want it badly enough."

"But what about my family—or more particularly, what about the way my father has treated you in the past? How do we get past such things?"

"Your father is easy. He'll accept me with open arms as soon as he understands that I'm as much a blue blood as he is, and not the penniless nobody he's taken me for. Because he has yet to develop a mind of his own, your brother Victor will do likewise.

"Andrew will shake my hand and wish me luck, because he knows I'm going to need it with such a hellion for a wife, and also because we like and respect one another. Your grandparents will not be surprised, not by anything they learn. They see much more than we give them credit for. Your mother will realize that I make you happy, and that will be enough for her."

"And Simon? It's as you said yesterday. How do we explain such a complicated past to him?"

He dropped a kiss on her head. Her hair smelled of grass and vanilla and the rich earth of Tuscany. "With Simon we will be patient and tell him only as much as he asks to know, and only when the time is right. For the present, we will simply be a family of three forging new bonds. But he is strong and courageous like his mother. When he is ready to hear how we came together, he will bear the truth bravely."

"I'm not so brave," she said in a muffled voice. "If it weren't for Corinna, I'd still be dithering about telling you the truth. You were right to call me a coward."

"You are the bravest woman I know, my lovely Stephanie."

"You're not disappointed in me?" She looked up at him from beneath the fringe of her long eyelashes.

He shook his head. "We've wasted enough time mired in past mistakes. It's time to move on to a better tomorrow. *Te amo*, Stephanie, and that's what matters."

She let out a long, trembling sigh. "I love you, too."

He looked around. Neat rows of grapevines climbed up the hillside opposite. The long grass had stained her dress and she had a smudge of dirt on her nose. A farm cart rumbled along the road toward them, stirring up a cloud of summer dust. The worker perched high on the seat was whistling. He had a dog sitting next to him.

"This isn't how I'd pictured it happening," Matteo said, "but when the moment is right, a man must act." He pulled her to her feet, then dropped to one knee before her and held her hands. "Stephanie Leyland-Owen, will you marry me? Will you live with me and let me love you 'til death do part us?"

She bit her lip and a tear splashed down her face to land on the back of his hand. "*Sì*," she said. "I'd be honored to be your wife."

He stood up and pulled her into his arms. "I have not kissed you in far too long," he told her, and brought his mouth down on hers.

She tasted of paradise. Of all the heated scents of summer in Italy, and the cool northern winters of her homeland. She tasted of forever.

The cart rumbled to a stop. The worker grinned and raised his thumb in approval. "*Viva l'amore!*" he shouted.

"*Viva l'amore,*" Stephanie echoed, her smile tremulous. "*Viva* you and me, Matteo."

"*Sì*," he said. "*Per eternità, la mia bella.*"

CHAPTER THIRTEEN

ON HER wedding morning, they came together in her suite at the *Villa Valenti,* the way women do, to help her get ready, and it didn't matter that they barely knew each other. They were mothers, and they wanted this day to be unforgettable—for her, for them, for the man already waiting in the chapel, and for the son he'd chosen to be his best man.

She didn't wear a long white gown with a sweeping train, or a lace veil held in place with a pearl tiara. This was not, after all, her first wedding, nor could she, by any stretch of the imagination, pass herself off as a virgin bride. Instead, she chose champagne silk kissed with the faintest blush of pink dawn, with a portrait neckline, and a full skirt which fell from a narrow fitted waist to whisper in soft folds around her ankles. Her shoes were satin, the same color as her dress, with elegant, three inch heels so that she had only to tilt up her face a little to look her husband in the eye as they exchanged their vows, and to receive his kiss to seal their union.

Of course, a dress and shoes weren't quite enough, not even with the addition of a nosegay of champagne bud roses secured by a wide satin ribbon.

"This," *Signora* De Luca said, presenting her with a wide-brimmed lace hat trimmed with exquisite silk roses, "is what I wore at Matteo's baptism. If you would like to wear it today—"

Delighted, Stephanie exclaimed, "Something old, and so beautiful! I'm honored, *Signora* De Luca!"

"No more of the *Signora, cara!* Today, I become your

182

suocera, your mother-in-law, and you become the daughter I always longed for—*la mia nuora.* So, *per favore,* call me *Madre.*'' She exchanged a warm smile with Stephanie's mother. "We will share our children and double our blessings, *sì,* Vivienne?''

Close to tears, Vivienne nodded. "In case I haven't said so a dozen times before, I'm so grateful you and Matteo found each other again, Stephanie. All I've ever wanted is to see you happy. But never in my wildest dreams did I think you and your father would arrive at the kind of understanding you've reached in the last two months. He's very proud of you, and has enormous respect for Matteo. Even though you'll be making your home here in Italy, please visit us often. We all want very much to be part of your new family.''

"Well, praise heaven, a family at last!'' Stephanie's grandmother said. "Don't go all weepy on us, Vivienne, you'll ruin your mascara. Stephanie, darling girl, I have something you may borrow just for today, although you will, one day, inherit it.'' She opened a navy velvet jeweler's case and took out a pair of pink diamond earrings. "Your grandfather gave these to me on our wedding day and it's only fitting that you should wear them on yours. They go very well with your lovely dress, don't you think?''

"I think Mother's not the only one about to ruin her mascara,'' Stephanie said, managing a smile even though her throat ached with an overload of emotion. "Thank you, Grandmother! I'll take very good care of them.''

"As Matteo will take very good care of you,'' *Nonna* decreed, presenting her with a handsome blue leather photograph album engraved in gold with the De Luca family crest, the date, and Stephanie and Matteo's initials. "Which is why I am giving you this, so that, starting today, you may begin recording the many good years ahead. There you have it, *cara mia:* something old, something blue and something borrowed. Only something new is missing.''

"And I took care of that," Vivienne said. "I bought you this, for your honeymoon, Stephanie." She produced a long, flat box in which a delicate lace and chiffon peignoir, extravagantly beribboned, nestled between layers of tissue paper. "Every bride should have at least one utterly impractical item in her trousseau and I know you're too down-to-earth to have indulged in anything as fanciful as this. Shall I put it in your suitcase?"

"Oh, please do!" Stephanie said, laughing. "Mother, I had no idea you were such a romantic."

A knock sounded at the sitting room door.

"I expect that's Bruce, come to walk her to the chapel," her grandmother said, ushering the women from the bedroom. "Come along, my dears, let's not delay the proceedings. Stephanie needs a moment alone with her father, and although it's one thing for a bride to be fashionably late, it's quite another for her to leave her guests wondering if she plans to show up at all."

"So, after you and Mom are married, does that make me your son?"

Matteo bent down to adjust the knot in Simon's pearl-gray tie, and secure the white rose boutonniere in the lapel of his morning suit jacket. "Very much so," he said. "You will be my son in every way."

"And I can call you 'Dad'?"

"I wouldn't have it any other way, *caro.* I want the whole world to know we are father and son."

"Do I get to be called Simon De Luca, instead of Simon Leyland-Owen?"

"Indeed, yes. As we explained to you yesterday, your mother and I have completed formal adoption arrangements. You are a true De Luca in every sense of the word.''

''I forgot you'd told me about that.'' Simon's face lit up with mischievous glee. ''We had fun yesterday, didn't we? I got to stay up late and dance with my new *Nonna*. Even Grandfather was smiling. I heard Great-Grandmommy say he's a lot easier to be around when he's had a snootful of champagne.''

Stifling a burst of laughter, Matteo turned away and made a mental note to watch what he said when his son was within hearing range. But *Signora* Anna's remark was right on target. Bruce Leyland had shown himself almost pathetically eager to please at last night's rehearsal dinner, being fulsomely attentive to *Madre* and *Nonna*, clapping Matteo fondly on the back, and making a lengthy speech, formally welcoming him to the family.

A different tune from the one he'd been playing two months ago! When he'd first heard Matteo was Simon's father, he'd threatened to disown the boy. Everything had changed overnight, though, when he also learned the man he considered beneath contempt owned the villa in which he was staying, had a pedigree a mile long, and could buy and sell the Leylands with pocket change, if he so chose. Suddenly, claiming a De Luca as a son-in-law was something to brag about.

Victor had followed suit, even going so far as to volunteer to be his best man, an offer Matteo had refused. What, did the man think he had no *real* friends, not to mention cousins, who'd be more than happy to fill the role? But Victor was, after all, Stephanie's brother, and therefore to be accorded civility, if nothing else. So Matteo had pointed out as gracefully as possible that he'd chosen his son to stand beside him on his wedding day.

''Do you have the ring, Simon?''

Simon patted his pocket. ''Yep. Right here.''

"And you know what to do when *Padre* Agnolo asks for it?"

"Yep. Give it to him, not you."

"And if I look a little pale, as if I'm afraid of what I'm letting myself in for?"

"You're never afraid," his son said, hooting with mirth. "You could kill a bear with one hand. Two bears, even! My mom won't scare you, not ever!"

"That's my boy!" He resisted the urge to ruffle Simon's hair and settled instead for man-to-man grin, then cast a last look over the garden.

Long tables were set out under a blue and white striped canopy on the terrace. Champagne chilled in huge barrels of ice. A flock of imported help bustled back and forth, making certain everything was in order for the wedding luncheon. The sun was high, the sky a pure unclouded blue.

Beyond the grounds, the grapevines climbed in orderly rows up the hillsides, heavy with fruit waiting to be harvested. It would be a good year. The best yet.

"Okay, *amico*," he said, taking his son's hand. "Let's get ourselves to the chapel. It wouldn't do to keep the bride waiting."

They were there already, filling the pews—his cousins, his friends. Jacomo and Andrew giving him the thumbs-up sign as he took his place before the altar. Corinna, her eyes just a little regretful, but her smile heartfelt. His mother and grandmother, shining with happiness for him. Stephanie's mother and grandmother, exchanging warm glances with his, the bond between them already strong. Her grandfather, the old grief which had marked his features for so long replaced by a serene acceptance. Victor being...Victor.

On a signal from the priest, the organist segued from

Bach to Pachelbel's Canon, at which the congregation rose and turned to watch as Stephanie made her entrance. Matteo had heard that brides were supposed to look radiant; had even seen a few who merited such a description. But never had he beheld anything to compare with his Stephanie as she made her way down the short aisle to his side.

Quite simply, she shimmered from the inside out. Was so luminous with joy and beauty that he refused even to blink, because to do so would have cheated him, however briefly, of the sight of her. And had to blink anyway, because raw emotion rose up to threaten his vision with the blur of tears.

He would remember this moment until his dying day, he vowed. He would love this woman as no man had ever loved before. *Per eternità.*

"Hey," he said, when at last she stood beside him.

She smiled, and his heart swelled. "Hey, yourself."

"Te amo."

"I love you, too."

It was enough. It was everything. Taking her hand, he turned to the family priest. "Marry us, *Padre,*" he said. "Make my beautiful bride my wife."

REQUEST YOUR FREE BOOKS!

HARLEQUIN *Presents*®

2 FREE NOVELS PLUS 2 FREE GIFTS!

PASSION GUARANTEED SEDUCTION

HARLEQUIN *Presents*

We're delighted to announce that

A Mediterranean Marriage

is taking place—and you are invited!

Imagine blue skies, an azure sea, a beautiful landscape
and the hot sun. What a perfect place to get married!
But although all ends well for these couples, their
route to happiness is filled with emotion and passion.

Follow their journey in the latest book
from this inviting miniseries.

BLACKMAILED
BY DIAMONDS,
BOUND BY MARRIAGE

by Sarah Morgan, #2598

Available this January!

Look out for more *A Mediterranean Marriage* stories
coming soon in Harlequin Presents!